Lure of the Bear

Aloha Shifters: Jewels of the Heart

Book 3

by Anna Lowe

Editing by Lisa A. Hollett

Covert art by Kim Killion

Contents

Other books in this series

Aloha Shifters - Jewels of the Heart

Lure of the Dragon (Book 1)

Lure of the Wolf (Book 2)

Lure of the Bear (Book 3)

Lure of the Tiger (Book 4)

Love of the Dragon (Book 5)

visit www.annalowebooks.com

Free Books

Get your free e-books now!

Sign up for my newsletter at *annalowebooks.com* to get three free books!

- *Desert Wolf*: Friend or Foe (Book 1.1 in the Twin Moon Ranch series)

- *Off the Charts* (the prequel to the Serendipity Adventure series)

- *Perfection* (the prequel to the Blue Moon Saloon series)

Chapter One

"No!" Hunter roared, lashing out at his attacker.

He stared into the night, coiled for action. But there was no one, and no sound but that of his own haggard breath. Sweat trickled down his neck, and his fists clenched the sheets as he sat up in bed.

"Shit." He flopped back and stared at the ceiling. Another nightmare.

He kept his eyes wide open, because that nightmare went way back to the ugliest part of his past, and he really didn't want to revisit it any more than he already had. He'd been just a cub, but it was all clear as a bell. The taste of salt water. The sound of his own panicked cries. The force of incessant waves that pushed his mother's body up the shore.

His jaw clenched so tightly, the joint popped. Then he threw back the sheets and walked stiffly to the porch, avoiding his own reflection in the windowpanes. He already knew he had dark circles under his eyes, that his hair was askew and his beard badly in need of a trim. He barely cared — except he'd been brought up better than that.

He sighed, watching the first rays of pink light peek through the swaying palms of the estate. After breakfast, he'd clean up and do his family proud, as he had for the past ten-plus years, both in private and as a soldier. But right now...

Hunter stood quietly, willing the sun to hurry up and chase away the night. Bear shifters were normally late risers, but the sun couldn't rise fast enough for him these days.

A run. What he needed was a good, hard run. That would clear his head. The question was whether to do so in human or bear form.

1

Bear, his inner grizzly said. *Let me out.*

Hunter closed his eyes and tried to convince himself there would be no harm in that.

No one will see, his bear said. *I promise.*

Hunter scuffed the wooden slats of the porch, hating that the thought even entered his mind. But the danger of being spotted as a bear had been so firmly beaten into him as a child, a cold chill went down his spine.

He lumbered slowly down the stairs.

I have every right to shift. I need to shift.

In truth, he was desperate to shift. For the past three weeks, he'd kept his bear locked in solitary confinement. But there was no denying that side of his soul, no matter how hard he tried.

No one will see, his bear swore. *We're safe here on Koa Point.*

He gave in at last, dropping to all fours and letting his bear take over. Then he gave his thick fur a good shake, sniffed the sea breeze, and rolled.

Stop that, you idiot, he barked at his bear.

But it feels so good to be me again, the beast cried.

It did feel good. The cool earth under the pads of his feet. The raw power in his limbs. The rich scents of Maui, amplified by his keen sense of smell.

He set off, working out the stiffness in his joints. His cottage was located near the entry gate of the estate where he and his band of Special Forces brothers lived. He crossed the perfectly groomed lawn and passed the long line of garages, running faster and faster, trying to outrun his own demons.

Most times, Hunter wasn't the fastest shifter living at Koa Point. Cruz, the tiger shifter, was lightning-quick over short distances. Boone, the wolf, could beat any of them over a mile. The two dragons, Silas and Kai, could soar through the sky at incredible speeds. As for Hunter — well, he could call up a pretty impressive sprint, but speed wasn't his strength.

And yet, three weeks ago, he'd outrun everyone to save the woman he loved. And he'd succeeded. He'd tackled the rogue wolf leaping at her just in time and mauled the beast to death.

Killing never felt good, but that time, it almost did — until the moment he'd looked up and seen Dawn backing away in horror. His destined mate, rejecting him.

He hammered along, making a big loop of the estate. Six acres didn't make for too long a circuit, and within minutes, he was racing along the beach. He nearly turned inland again, but he forced himself to stop and absorb the view. Venus was slipping toward the horizon, and the colors of daybreak were deepening. A beautiful scene, right?

He gritted his teeth and inched closer to the water, far enough to let the waves lick his feet. The surf was up, pounding into the reef that protected Koa Point's strip of beach. Something bobbed in the shallows, and for a moment, his heart jumped to his throat.

It's only a piece of driftwood, he told his bear.

A piece of driftwood that brought back the nightmares in which his mother's coarse fur was clumped with salt water and blood.

He shook his thick pelt. *That was in Alaska, a long time ago. This is Maui, and the sun is rising, not setting.*

He forced himself to endure the gritty touch of salt water on his fur, not quite sure whether that was a punishment or therapy.

It's bound to be another beautiful day, his inner bear tried, but the words felt hollow. Empty — like him.

He walked back up the beach and moved inland to the more soothing world of greens and browns, where he could walk through the foliage and relish the tickle of leaves over his spine. He sniffed as he walked, inhaling the rich earth and surrounding scents. Sweet hibiscus, exquisite honohono flowers, and sugarbush. Maybe if he walked long enough, some of the peace of the place would rub off on his soul.

The sound of a woman's giggle drifted through the trees, answered by the lower murmur of a man, both of them happy and serene. That had to be Nina and Boone, celebrating the new day with a kiss. Well, probably with a lot more than a kiss, if Hunter knew those two. But who could blame them? Destined mates had every right to love, to truly live.

3

Hunter drew in a slow breath and pulled his teeth over his lower lip. Why did their happiness set off such an ache in his chest? He ought to be happy for Boone and Nina.

I am happy for them, his bear insisted. *I just wish...*

Hunter let out a gruff snort. A man could wish a lot of things, but he couldn't change what he was.

He set off on another loop of the estate, running hard.

It's only a matter of time before Nina and Boone have kids, you know, his bear murmured.

Hunter scowled. He'd be thrilled for his buddy, but it would kill him to know he'd never have that joy.

We can be uncles, he tried telling his inner beast. *That will be fun, too.*

His bear growled out loud. *Not the same thing. Maybe we should leave.*

According to Boone, there was a new bear clan starting up in Arizona at a funky place called the Blue Moon Saloon. Maybe he could start fresh there. That, or he could go back to his roots in Alaska. Someplace where he wouldn't be tortured daily by the sight of his destined mate — and she wouldn't be tortured by the sight of him, the monster she loathed.

But just like every other time he entertained the notion, he discarded it. There was no way he could get on a plane and leave his destined mate. No way.

He ran on and on, losing track of how many laps of the property he'd pounded over. He ran until the sun wasn't just inching over the horizon but climbing fast. Only then, panting and soaked with sweat, did he turn back to his cottage.

"Morning," a voice called, making his head jerk up. Kai was sitting on Hunter's porch, watching the brilliant colors drain out of the sky.

Hunter grimaced. Kai was his oldest friend, but he had that *I'm here to cheer you up* look on his face.

"Beautiful sunrise, huh?" Kai murmured.

Hunter shrugged. Every sunrise was beautiful on Maui. If only the light didn't glint off the windows of his house and catch his reflection like that. All that fur. Claws. Fangs. Weapons of destruction, at least in the eyes of most humans, including the one he cared about most.

The voice of Georgia Mae, his foster mother, drifted through his mind. *Sweetheart, you are who you are. And you're wonderful.*

Dawn doesn't think I'm wonderful, his bear whispered, hanging his head.

"How you doing? Okay?" Kai asked.

Not really, no. Hunter took a deep breath and forced himself to face the new day by shifting back to human form.

"I'm fine," he grumbled, cracking his knuckles.

"Tessa's making some oatmeal for you," Kai said. "A new recipe she's trying out for her cookbook."

Hunter looked at the sky. Tessa's cookbook was about grilling, not breakfast, and he knew it. She was just trying to shake him out of his funk.

Despite the fact that he'd lost his appetite weeks ago, he nodded. "That's nice. I'll be there soon." What else could he do?

Kai stood and motioned to the driveway. "By the way, we reworked the plan for today. Boone is going to drop me off at the airport to sign for the new helicopter, and he can pick you up at the resort on the way back."

Hunter blinked a few times, trying to recall what that was all about.

"The Rolls, remember?" Kai prompted.

Oh, right. That. Hunter was supposed to deliver the Rolls Royce — one of the estate owner's many fancy cars — from Koa Point to the exclusive Kapa'akea resort, where it was being leased for a celebrity wedding of some kind.

"Don't make such a face," Kai said, borrowing a line from Georgia Mae. "You need to get out a little."

"I need to be left alone," Hunter growled.

"And you need to talk to Dawn," Kai added as if Hunter hadn't just spoken.

He scoffed. "Sure. Maybe even invite her out to dinner with me in bear form."

"Dinner. Great idea." Kai nodded. "In human form. You get cleaned up, show her what a great guy you are..."

Hunter stomped past Kai and into the house.

"Come on, Hunter. You've known her since you were fourteen."

As if he didn't know that. Hunter remembered the very day, the very hour he'd first met Dawn Meli, fifteen years ago. He'd known she was his destined mate from the start, but she sure hadn't. Besides, she had been the gorgeous, homecoming queen type, and he had been the gangly new kid in town. Hell, he still felt like the gangly new kid in town, at least around her.

"Hunter, she knows you. She likes you. The fact that she didn't turn us in after that mess with Kramer and his mercenaries proves it."

Hunter turned on the shower, trying to drown Kai out. That Dawn hadn't exposed their shifter secret after that fight probably had more to do with the fact that the policewoman was still reeling from the experience. And as for her liking him...

She does like us, his bear whispered. *Remember how she looked at us?*

Hunter remembered all the occasions time had stopped when their eyes met, when something in his heart fluttered and his pulse skipped. Dawn's cheeks had always flushed, and the way her eyes lit up on seeing him had given him hope that maybe, just maybe...

He scrubbed his face, trying to forget, because the memory of her horrified expression was fresher.

"You guys are made for each other, Hunter. Her last name even means honey."

Hunter frowned. *Meli* did mean honey in Hawaiian. He used to believe it was a sign, but now, it just seemed like another cruel twist of fate.

"If that's not destiny, I don't know what is." Kai persisted, calling over the noise of the shower. "Damn it, Hunter. You can't deny yourself your destined mate. I tried with Tessa, but it was impossible."

Hunter closed his eyes and let the steam of the shower lock the world away. What was impossible was the notion of Dawn ever accepting him, and he knew it.

Chapter Two

Driving to town was easy enough, especially once Hunter drove past the spot where Dawn — Officer Meli — usually parked her squad car. The fact that she wasn't there was cause for both relief and concern. Relief in not having to face her, and concern because Dawn rarely broke her routine.

She's a lot like a bear that way, his inner beast murmured.

It was only a short drive to the Kapa'akea resort, and Hunter spent most of it wondering where Dawn might be, what she was doing, and whether she was thinking of him. All that instead of him listening in satisfaction as the Rolls purred along. It was only the appreciative whistle of the guard at the resort gate that pulled him back to the business at hand.

"Sweet car," the portly man said, making a full lap around the Rolls.

Hunter tapped his fingers on the steering wheel and growled under his breath. The guy better not touch the wax job he'd spend most of the previous day on, or—

He caught himself there. Or what? What would he do? Turn into a bear and scare the guy out of his wits?

He gripped the steering wheel tighter and ground his teeth until the guard stepped away to check a clipboard.

"Let me guess," a second guard said. "It's been leased for the Vanderpelt wedding."

Hunter nodded curtly.

"Man, those people are pulling out all the stops," the first guard said, raising the gate. "You know where to go?"

Hunter nodded as he drove through. Yeah, he knew his way around the exclusive resort, having worked a few jobs there as private security. But man, he'd never seen the place bustle with quite so much activity. A huge tent was being erected on one end of the polo field, and an outdoor seating area was slowly taking shape. A photographer was setting up lights by the gazebo, and the air buzzed with the sound of a chainsaw as a man sculpted a huge block of ice. Hunter shook his head. The Kapa'akea resort hosted several spare-no-expense weddings each year, but this appeared to be the event of the century.

An eager valet bounded up to the Rolls Royce as Hunter approached the main building. "I'll be happy to take it from here."

Hunter waved the guy off. That valet barely looked nineteen — and not the kind of nineteen Hunter had once been with a year of military service under his belt. Nope. Only three people drove that car: Hunter, the car's owner — a man he'd never seen, and the appropriately gray-haired chauffeur hired by the resort for big-money gigs.

"Second to last garage from the end, right?" he asked.

The kid looked crestfallen, so Hunter sighed and nodded to the passenger seat. "Want a ride?"

The valet lit up like it was Christmas and slid into the passenger seat, spinning his head around.

"Wow. I mean, this is a great car. I mean... Wow. A real Rolls Royce."

Hunter drove slowly down the lane. "Big event, huh?"

The valet bounced in his seat. "Bigger than big. I saw her today."

"Saw who?"

"Her. Regina Vanderpelt."

The name rang a bell, but Hunter couldn't figure out why.

"The Regina Vanderpelt. You know her, right? She's totally famous."

Hunter rubbed his freshly trimmed beard. "Famous for what?"

"Um... well... She's famous for being famous, I guess. Rich and famous. She's always in all the magazines. It's the wedding of the century, and it's happening here."

Hunter made a mental note to stay clear of the place for the next week. Was Regina Vanderpelt the bratty heiress who featured regularly on the covers of tabloids? A sex scandal here, a high-profile breakup there.

Yeah, he'd definitely keep clear of the place. He parked, locked up, and triple-checked the doors.

The valet laughed. "The car is safe, man. Besides, it's insured, right?"

Of course, the car was insured. But Hunter had put enough time into keeping that V12 engine safe from the harsh elements of the tropics to care about a lot more than replacement value.

Before handing the key over, he gave the kid a long, withering look. "No one touches this car but the chauffeur. Got it?"

"Got it. Got it," the guy gulped.

Hunter hung on to the key when the kid reached for it, reinforcing the unspoken warning before finally letting go.

"Want a ride back to the gate?" the valet offered, waving to a golf cart.

Hunter scowled. He would barely fit in that ridiculous contraption, for one thing, and he was still relishing the smooth ride of the Rolls, for another. But he didn't want to spend a minute longer than he had to in the ritzy, overpriced resort, so he nodded and folded himself into the front seat.

"They've invited more than five hundred guests," the valet shouted as they drove past the ice sculptor. The chainsaw was going full blast, spewing bits of ice as far as the road. "Every penthouse on this side of the island is booked. I swear, the flower bill alone would pay my entire student loan."

Hunter snorted. He'd never had much money, and he probably never would. But what he did have, he wouldn't spend on flowers. Well, not on flowers that would never grow in the wild and sway with a breeze.

A memory zipped through his mind — one of the few he had that went way back. Back to when he'd been a tiny cub, when his mother seemed huge and the world seemed even bigger. He remembered the two of them walking in bear form through a meadow of wildflowers that tickled his belly and nose until he sneezed. One of those perfect spring days in Alaska made all the more beautiful by a long, hard winter and by his mother's lighthearted chuckles. An innocent day when life had seemed so sweet and serene.

"Some people have it all, huh?" the valet murmured, waving toward an oncoming truck from Maui's most exclusive catering company.

Hunter blinked a few times and took a long, deep breath. Yeah, some people had it all. He'd had everything a bear could wish for until it had all been ripped away. Over the past few months, he'd even been entertaining fantasies that he could live that great a life again by winning over his mate. If he had Dawn, he wouldn't need much else. He would have his mate and a lot of love. He could wake every morning by her side and spend every night holding her close. He could—

He bit his lip, cutting the fantasies off there. He would never have that. He'd blown his chance the day he had exposed his bear side to Dawn in the worst possible way.

What was I supposed to do? That rogue wolf was going to kill her, his bear cried.

"Well, I guess we'll see you next week," the valet said, dropping him by the front gate.

Hunter pried himself out of the golf cart, murmuring his thanks as those words bounced around his mind. Next week would be just as miserable as this week and the week after that. Somehow, he had to reconcile himself to the idea of a life without his mate.

A beep sounded, making everyone look up, and Hunter caught a flash of red racing in from the main road.

"Him again," the guard muttered at the sight of Boone zipping up in the Ferrari.

The wolf shifter flashed one of his winning grins as he pulled up. "Hop in."

"Hop?" Hunter sighed as he squeezed into the low-slung car. "Couldn't you have driven the Land Rover?"

"No time to waste," Boone said as he raced back to the main road and made the left turn for home. "It took forever to take Kai to the airport. I need to get back to my mate and—" He cut himself off there. "Oh. I mean. . . "

Hunter looked at his feet as an awkward silence fell over the car — silence broken a few minutes later when a helicopter buzzed overhead.

Boone beeped and waved through the open roof of the Ferrari. "There's Kai with the new chopper."

"Keep your eyes on the road," Hunter muttered as the car's speed inched up.

"No problem." Boone jerked the wheel to straighten out.

"You need to slow down, too."

"Nah. Like I said, no time to waste."

Hunter braced his arms on the dashboard as the scenery flashed by. "Boone. . . "

"I got this, man. We're nearly there."

They were nearly to the curve staked out by Officer Dawn Meli of the Maui police, too. If she was on duty, she was bound to pull Boone over, and Hunter wasn't ready to face her yet.

"Boone. . . "

"Live a little, man," Boone said, racing around the corner.

Hunter peeked right, and his heart pounded at the sight of Dawn's white-and-blue cruiser.

She's back! His bear practically leaped for joy. *She's back! Maybe she'll pull us over.*

The Ferrari raced on, and Hunter kept his eyes glued to the side mirror, waiting for the flash of police lights.

"Hey," Boone murmured, slowing down. "She's not pulling me over?"

The joy that had burst into Hunter's soul slowly seeped out. Dawn wasn't pulling them over. She was avoiding him, just as he'd been avoiding her.

Boone slowed even more, then signaled a left turn onto a private drive.

Hunter made a face. "Wait. What are you doing? This isn't the driveway to Koa Point."

Boone put the Ferrari into reverse, scattering dirt as he headed back the way they'd come. "I'm going back."

Hunter dug his nails into the dashboard. "What?"

"I have a right be pulled over, damn it," Boone said with a sly look on his face.

"I thought you were in a rush to get back to your mate."

"I am, but this is as important."

"Boone," Hunter growled, to no avail. He sank as low in his seat as he could when Boone drove past the squad car again. "Don't do this, Boone."

"Time to man up, bear." Boone chuckled as he turned the car yet again. He drove directly to the pullout and parked next to the squad car, putting Hunter window-to-window with a wide-eyed Officer Meli.

His breath caught, and his blood warmed.

Mate, his bear hummed. *My perfect mate.*

She was perfect in every possible way. Her fine features, her glossy black hair. Her dark, searching eyes. Back in school, everyone had predicted that Dawn would win modeling contracts and hit it big thanks to her gorgeous blend of Polynesian, Asian, and Caucasian features, but she'd shunned the suggestion and gone to law school instead. And after law school, she'd surprised everyone again by going into law enforcement.

My mate always does the unexpected, his bear said with a dreamy sigh.

"Officer Meli!" Boone called cheerily.

Hunter closed his eyes, savoring a whiff of her flowery scent.

"Mr. Hawthorne," she said in an icy voice that warmed and wavered when she looked at Hunter. "Mr. Bjornvald."

Hunter snapped his eyes open again. "Dawn," he whispered.

"You didn't pull me over," Boone said.

"No, I didn't." Her dark eyes were hard and unamused, but when they strayed toward Hunter, they flickered — and not in fear. More like. . . recognition. Maybe even warmth.

I told you! his bear cried. *I told you she loves us.*

But why would she? Humans didn't know about destined mates.

Deep inside, our mate knows, his bear insisted. *Destiny told her, too.*

"I was speeding," Boone said.

14

Officer Meli's brow furrowed. "I decided to let it go this once."

"But speeding is unlawful. I really think you ought to give me a ticket."

She pushed open the door of her squad car and stood with her hands on her hips. "Mr. Hawthorne, I decide when I issue a ticket. Is that clear?"

How she managed to look beautiful and menacing at the same time, Hunter didn't know.

She'd make a great bear, his inner beast sighed.

"Yes, ma'am," Boone said, putting on his best chagrined schoolboy look as he swung the car door open.

Officer Meli went into a defensive stance, one arm hovering over the weapon at her hip. "Hold it right there."

Boone stood and stretched. "Sorry. An old army injury is suddenly flaring up. I need to walk it off."

"Old army what?" Hunter murmured, stepping out of the car. Boone had his share of war wounds, as did every member of their Special Forces unit, but as a quick-healing shifter, Boone didn't suffer any long-term effects. What was he up to?

Dawn spun. "Whoa. You hold it, too."

Hunter threw his hands up as Boone faked a grimace and limped up the dirt track that led from the pullout toward the West Maui mountains. "I'll be fine in a few minutes. Don't worry."

"Worry?" Dawn didn't sound the least bit concerned. Her eyes darted from Boone's back to Hunter's face.

Hunter pushed the car door closed and leaned against it, keeping his hands in plain view. Christ, what was he thinking, hopping out of the car like that?

I was thinking, get closer to my mate, his bear murmured inside.

We'll scare her, he hissed back.

Boone's footsteps crunched over gravel then faded into the distance, leaving Hunter and Dawn alone. He scrubbed a hand over his jaw, wondering what to do.

Time to man up, bear. Boone's words echoed through his mind, and a few awkward seconds later, he finally spoke. "Look—"

"Look," Dawn said at exactly the same time.

They both stopped cold, staring at each other.

Hunter scuffed the dirt with his boot. "Ladies first."

"No, you first," she insisted, crossing her arms.

Right. If only he knew what to say other than, *Look.*

Say, I love you, his bear tried.

Hunter shook his head. No way was he opening with that line.

Say, you can trust me.

Hunter shoved his hands deeper into his pockets. Damn it, why was it that a bear who didn't fear anything had to be so scared of uttering a few words?

Then kiss her.

He gritted his teeth. Much as he'd like to, that wouldn't work either.

She sighed. "Tongue-tied as ever, I see."

Hunter looked up. Another woman might have laced the words with scorn, but not Dawn. If anything, there was a hint of fondness in her voice. Or was he imagining things?

They stood facing each other for a full minute, speechless. Any second, Hunter figured, his brief stint in heaven would be over — just being close to Dawn was heaven — so he imprinted the moment onto his mind. A wisp of hair had strayed out of her single braid, and the sea breeze twirled it exactly the way he fantasized about doing himself. The sun shone from high overhead, casting her face into smooth fields of shadow and light. When her gaze wandered to his chest then snapped back to his eyes, her throat bobbed with a tiny swallow.

Hunter gulped, too, because it was happening again. That magical aura that overwhelmed him every time he came close to his mate. The sensation that rose out of nowhere and wound around the two of them, locking the outside world away. The hum of passing cars, the scratch of insects in the surrounding scrub — all sound faded until the only thing Hunter heard was the beat of his heart. All he saw was the faint rise and fall of

Dawn's shoulders with each deep breath. Her face was bright and clear, but everything else grew blurry, as if the sun was slowly turning a lens and focusing all its light on her.

This is your mate. A whisper came from somewhere deep in the earth. *This is your destiny.*

Dawn's eyes shone brighter, and she leaned forward slightly.

She needs you as much as you need her, the voice said, coaxing him along.

A yellow butterfly fluttered between them, but even that was a blur. Nothing mattered but Dawn.

His lips moved with words he couldn't form, and when his hand brushed hers, she didn't jerk away.

"Hunter," she whispered.

The stern police officer was gone, as was the woman who had been shocked by the grizzly she'd seen a few weeks ago. All that remained was the girl he'd once known, fresh and eager and leaning so close, his body burned with need.

Hunter leaned down — without thinking, because instinct had taken over, and he was powerless to do anything but react — and hovered an inch away from her lips. His eyelids drooped, and his focus narrowed on the fine line of her lips. Dawn tilted her head slightly, and she rolled forward on her toes, closing the tiny space between them.

Then, *zoom!* A truck rushed by, buffeting them both with its wake, whipping reality back in.

Chapter Three

Dawn snapped her eyes open and blinked a few times. Holy cow. What was she doing? If she had to write up an incident report later, she would have no idea where to start.

One second, I was getting ready to tell him to back off, and the next, we were nearly kissing.

She could practically hear the snickers of her fellow officers. A good thing there were no witnesses there on the side of the road this glorious day in West Maui.

Not that it had been a glorious day when it started. She'd been grumpy and off-kilter all morning, as she had been for the past few weeks. No matter how much tai chi or yoga she tried, she couldn't settle down. Every morning, she set off on a punishing run, and every evening, she spent ages tidying her perfectly clean bungalow, adjusting the bookshelves so the spines lined up just right and fidgeting with picture frames that weren't actually askew, compulsively seeking the order and control her soul craved.

Control that always went out the window whenever Hunter was concerned. She'd never been so frustrated or confused.

But when he got close — as close as just then — all her doubts and fears fled, and she was immersed in a radiant world of comfort and bliss. Every nerve in her body took flight like the butterfly that had just flitted past, and her whole body tingled with glee.

All the man had to do was blink those impossibly long eyelashes, and she was a goner. Her, the don't-mess-with-me police officer who'd booked dozens of men twice her size, from heinous criminals to big, rowdy drunks and everything in be-

ANNA LOWE

tween. Yet somehow, she got all dreamy-eyed and off-focus when it came to Hunter.

Hunter, the man she'd secretly loved for years.

Part of her had already fast-forwarded into the kiss, and it actually hurt to imagine what she had just missed. She could have relived the one kiss she and Hunter had once shared, years ago — the only kiss she'd ever given freely to a man. She could have felt the soft pillow of his lips over hers and wrapped her arms slowly around his bulk. She could have felt Hunter pull her in gently, as he had that one perfect moment more than a decade ago under their secret waterfall. They had been teenagers, but even then, she had felt so sure that Hunter was the one.

Except, of course, that he'd abruptly stopped seeing her after that, and he'd shipped out with the army as soon as he graduated from high school. But ever since Hunter had returned to Maui after so many years away, she'd dreamed of kissing him again. Yes, she, Dawn Meli, had actually dreamed of kissing a man instead of harboring nightmares of desperately fighting one off.

Forget that ever happened, she reminded herself. *I can trust Hunter.*

Can't trust any man, a dark voice grumbled from the recesses of her mind.

The *man* part wasn't what made her step back at that point, because Hunter wasn't just a man. He had a secret, animal side capable of the most brutal acts. She'd seen the body count too recently to forget.

It all happened down at a secluded seaside property a few miles from Kihei. She'd responded to a report of strange noises and a fight — only to find Hunter and his friends standing amidst carnage like she'd never seen. There were bodies everywhere, and Dawn was about to demand an explanation when a huge wolf had barreled out of nowhere and leaped for her throat. She'd seen murder in the red shine of its eyes and the white flecks of foam on its huge fangs. She'd gotten one shot off, but the beast had barreled on. She thought she was a goner until another feral growl split the air. A bear — a huge grizzly

20

with fur the exact shade of Hunter's hair — caught the wolf and tore it to bits. Moments later, the bear hunched, moaned, and slowly transformed into a man. Hunter.

Hunter was a bear.

She'd almost called the incident in to police headquarters, but the beseeching look in Hunter's eyes convinced her to hear him out. Well, she heard his friend Boone out because Hunter, as usual, had been at a loss for words.

Shifters, Boone had explained. *We're all shifters. The dead men are shifters, too, like that wolf that attacked you.*

She might have dismissed his crazy claims had it not been for the dead wolf transforming to human form in front of her eyes.

I'm a wolf. Cruz is a tiger, Boone explained. *And Hunter is a grizzly.*

These aren't the bad guys, Officer, the sole woman on the scene had said. Nina was her name. *Please, let's hear them out.*

Dawn had heard them out. What choice did she have? And in the end, she'd gone against every vow she'd taken in law enforcement and decided not to call in the crime.

Why? Because she'd known Hunter as a kid. Because he and his friends exuded a sense of gruff honesty that spoke to something in her soul. Because how the hell would she ever explain what she'd seen? Hawaii had its share of shapeshifting tales — tales of men who could turn into sharks or women who turned into dragons and guarded clear mountain streams. But those were just stories, right?

Sure. Stories. Right.

Still, her heart had pleaded Hunter's case, and the discreet investigation she'd carried out afterward indicated that the dead men all shared ruthlessly criminal pasts. In the end, she couldn't help but think that justice had been served, if by unconventional means. So she'd laid the covered-up crime to rest and come to peace with her role in it. Well, mostly. But she couldn't get over the shifter part. She couldn't stop replaying the moment the bear transformed into Hunter — twisting, groaning, contorting...

21

But there they stood in the bright light of day, two tongue-tied humans filled with so much longing and pain.

Something stirred in the Ferrari, and she glanced in. It was just a sheet of paper, one of many that littered the back. Boone's speeding tickets, no doubt. She fought the urge to reach in and tidy them up. Instead, she turned back to Hunter — Hunter, the bear — and backed away.

His face fell.

"Hunter," she said, forcing herself to step closer again.

His eyes hit the ground, and his hands burrowed deeper into his pockets.

"Please, Hunter. Look at me," she whispered.

Slowly, he tipped his chin to meet her gaze. A world of pain and regret swirled in his chocolate brown eyes.

"I'd never hurt you, Dawn. If nothing else, please believe that."

Men made lots of promises. But Hunter, she believed.

"I know," she whispered. "It's just...just..." Now she was the one struggling for words. The zaps of electricity she'd always felt around Hunter were stronger than ever. A magnetic pull, an urge to sidle closer and let their bodies brush. How could she explain how strongly she was drawn to him — and how afraid she was of losing control?

"You've saved me two times now," she murmured. The first time was back in high school when... She halted the thought quickly. "And I appreciate it. More than I can say. But I'm still trying to swallow the bear part."

There, she'd said it. But Hunter looked glummer than ever, and it occurred to her what it must be like for him. As a person of mixed heritage, she'd endured a few racial slurs as a kid, though she'd come to embrace who she was.

Had Hunter? He couldn't help who he was, right?

But still — a bear?

She tried softening the unintended insult. "I mean, I should have guessed."

Hunter's thick eyebrows jumped up, and she couldn't hold back a tiny smile. She waved at him. "The size fits."

His face fell again, and she tapped him on the arm. "Hey. It's true. Bears are kind of quiet, too. Right?"

He nodded but didn't brighten one bit. And really, what was she trying to say? That she didn't mind him turning into a bear? He'd scared the hell out of her. Worse, he'd confirmed her theory that most men had a hidden, caveman side capable of terrible violence and awful deeds. Men waged wars and committed heinous crimes. Men raped and killed. Some even beat the people they professed to love. She'd gone into law to fight that kind of crime, then decided the police force was a better way to wage her own personal crusade.

Of course, there were decent men, too. But if Hunter could turn into a coldhearted killer, anyone could.

She stepped back again. Whatever she felt for Hunter, she couldn't give in to the pull. The heart had a way of tricking the mind, and she had to be vigilant. She had to remember who she was, too — an officer of the law. She'd already covered up a crime for Hunter's sake. If there was further trouble, she might have to report the man she loved, despite the consequences it could bring for him and his kind.

No, it was definitely better to stay single, clear-headed, and away from this man.

"I guess what I'm saying is, I just need some space. Okay?"

Hunter opened his mouth to say something, but the radio in her squad car squawked. "Unit 239, Unit 239. Come in, over."

She and Hunter stood staring at each other for another long minute before she whispered, "I have to go."

She didn't move, though, and the radio came on again. "Unit 239. Come in, over."

If it wasn't for Boone sauntering back down the trail, as cheerful as can be — and not limping in the slightest — she might have stayed rooted in place all day. There was so much more she needed to say. So much she needed Hunter to explain. But she couldn't — wouldn't — allow herself to go down that road.

She grabbed the handset. "Unit 239, over."

Hunter gave one last sad shake of the head and slid back into the Ferrari. When Boone revved the engine and peeled onto the highway with a squeal of the tires, Dawn kept her eye on the vehicle. Well, she kept an eye on Hunter. As he rushed out of sight — with Boone en route to breaking the speed limit yet again — something deep inside her ached, the way it always did when she and Hunter parted ways.

"The sergeant wants you back at headquarters for a special assignment, over."

Only part of Dawn's mind wondered what she was being reassigned to. The rest was still considering Hunter. What was it about him that pulled on her so? Did bear shifters have extra strong hormones or something?

"Unit 239, do you copy?" the dispatcher repeated a second later.

"Copy," Dawn sighed, watching Hunter disappear around the turn.

Chapter Four

Hunter gripped the door handle as Boone raced away.

"So, how did it go?" the wolf shifter asked.

Hunter just about showed his fangs. What did Boone expect him to say? *I think it will work out?* It would never work out between him and Dawn. And if he was honest with himself, things were better that way. The world of shifters was a dangerous one, and he'd already involved Dawn more than he had ever intended to.

If you were honest with yourself, you'd admit that we can't live without her, his bear growled.

Oh, he'd be happy to admit as much. But he had to think about Dawn, not himself.

Thankfully, Boone was quiet for the short drive back to Koa Point, where Hunter couldn't wait to lose himself in work. He maintained the estate's fleet of cars to perfection, but there was always something to check, or he could go back to restoring the 1971 Porsche 911 waiting in the back bay. Work was about the only thing that kept him sane.

But Silas, damn him, had other ideas. The second Hunter and Boone stepped out of the car, the tall dragon shifter who'd once headed their Special Forces unit strode up, pointing at him.

"We got a call for a new job," Silas said. "Security at the Kapa'akea resort."

Hunter ground his teeth. He'd just come from the resort, and he didn't have the focus to be an effective security guard at the moment. Not with his bear obsessing about his mate all the time.

Silas seemed to read his mind. "It's just what you need."

Hunter kicked the dirt. What he needed was his mate. Short of that, he needed the escape of the garage. Why wouldn't everyone leave him alone?

"Kai would do a better job," he grunted.

"Kai's going, too." Silas nodded. "They've hired the helicopter for the week."

Hunter wondered who *they* were.

"What about Boone?"

"Sorry, man. I'm working security at the surfing championships." The wolf shifter grinned.

Hunter nearly protested, but it did make sense. Happy-go-lucky Boone — who was doubly happy now that he'd found his destined mate, Nina — would fit right in at the surfing event.

"What about Cruz? He could do it."

"Cruz is on the job, too," Silas said as the tiger shifter prowled up, looking as unenthusiastic as Hunter felt. "You start in an hour, so get dressed and ship out."

Silas's tone left no room for argument, and an hour later, Hunter was back on the manicured grounds of the Kapa'akea resort with Cruz, both of them tugging on their ties and scowling deeply as Lorraine, a woman from hotel security, showed them around.

"Over there is the tent for the reception, and behind that is catering." She waved over the huge expanse of lush grass that separated the third hole of the golf course from the beach.

"Who's getting married?" Cruz grumbled.

"Regina somebody or other," Hunter sighed.

Lorraine turned and gaped. "Regina Vanderpelt. *The* Regina Vanderpelt." She looked from Cruz to Hunter and back to Cruz. "You know her, right?"

Hunter remembered what the valet had said earlier. *She's famous for being famous.*

"The one with the sex tape scandal?" Cruz yawned into the back of his hand.

Lorraine shushed him quickly. "We're not supposed to mention that. But, yes. The one with the sex tape scandal — and the drug scandal. The fashion-line-produced-by-child-labor-in-Bangladesh scandal, too. You name it, she's done it."

Funny, the clean-cut hotel employee sounded almost wistful as she described the bride.

Just the family name makes me suspicious, Cruz sniffed, shooting the words into Hunter's mind as all closely bonded shifters could. *Seriously — Vanderpelt?*

Hunter grimaced. From what he recalled, the family had made its fortune in oil. Which was bad enough, considering the toll the industry had taken on the wildest parts of Alaska.

Visions of his childhood jumped into his mind, and he forced himself to concentrate on the good parts instead of the bad. The evil men who'd taken away his loved ones were dead and gone. There was no need to dwell on them.

His bear growled inside. *Jericho Deroux...*

He closed his eyes, pushing the thought — and the name — out of his mind. A gentle breeze wafted over the manicured grounds, and the sweet fragrance of tropical flowers reminded him that he was living a whole new life in Maui. A good life. He had a great place to live alongside his shifter brothers. Even if the others weren't technically brothers, they had become as close as family — closer, even — through their years together in the military. So really, what else could a bear wish for?

His mate, a deep voice inside him growled.

He frowned, sniffing the air. Amidst the scent of sweat, tanning lotion, and flowers was the faintest whiff of... something he couldn't exactly place. He looked around, studying the scene for someone or something unusual.

You smell that? he asked Cruz.

Cruz shrugged, uninterested. *I smell trouble, that's for sure. All these humans...* He scowled.

Hunter nearly griped, *Of course they're all humans.* There were only a handful of shapeshifters on Maui, and he and Cruz knew every one.

He sniffed again. Was that the scent of shifter he'd picked up? It was so faint, he couldn't be sure, not even with his keen bear senses.

What? Cruz asked, catching his concern.

Not sure, he said, swinging his head, studying the shadows around the perimeter of the lawn. The grounds were

27

bustling with workers unloading equipment, setting out chairs, and studying plans. A scent that faint was hard to judge. It might not be a shifter at all.

"The wedding itself is going to be on the beach," Lorraine explained, deaf to their exchange. "And I swear, if these people could hire the weather, they would." She led Hunter and Cruz toward the shaded porch of the main building. "You two will be accountable to Armor Security, the firm hired to coordinate security for this event. We at the resort have our entire security force on call for the week, but Armor outnumbers us five-to-one, and they're calling the shots. Them and Veronica, the bride's personal assistant."

She pointed to a no-nonsense woman in a dress suit who tapped into a tablet and gestured to an electrician. Everything about the fifty-something-year-old said *professional* and *calm* — the opposite of the whirlwind approaching from the right.

"Uh-oh. Make way for Bridezilla," Lorraine whispered as a shrill cry broke out.

A young woman stomped up, and a path cleared like the waters parting before Moses.

"No, no, no! It's all wrong."

How anyone could move that fast on platform espadrilles, Hunter wasn't sure, but the young woman stormed along as intent as a tornado out to destroy everything in its path. She wore oversize sunglasses and a sheer, see-through top with a bright pink bikini underneath — all in all, the picture of a haughty supermodel, though the pinched look on her face made Hunter doubt she'd make a magazine cover for anything but her wealth or bratty escapades. A thick gold bracelet shone on her wrist, and her diamond earrings caught the sun. A string of exquisite pearls shimmered at her slim neck, and something purple flashed on her ring finger, catching Hunter's attention.

"Veronica!" she screeched.

Everyone in a hundred-foot radius cringed.

"Yes, Regina?" the personal assistant asked in a completely neutral tone.

Hunter wondered why rich girls always looked so underfed — and so unhappy.

"This is a disaster!" the bride-to-be announced.

Cruz shot Hunter a look. *Next time, we get the surf championship job.*

"Come and see," the young bride commanded, and everyone either lunged forward obediently or backed the hell away. Hunter and Cruz were the only two who held their ground. But when Hunter saw the bride headed to the garage he'd parked the Rolls Royce in earlier, he followed, too.

Regina stopped beside the vehicle and thrust her hands on her hips. "That is a disaster!"

Hunter stood beside Toby, the valet, who'd come along for the spectacle, and peeked into the garage. If Toby had messed with the Rolls, he'd kill him. But the vehicle gleamed in the sun, undamaged.

"What's wrong?" Veronica asked.

The haughty young woman ran a finger along the perfect wax job Hunter had spent hours on. "This is not the car I wanted."

Hunter pursed his lips. He'd never met someone who was picky about which Rolls Royce they drove as long as it was a Rolls.

"I want the one the Queen has," Regina sniffed. "Who brought me this piece of junk?"

Junk? Hunter's eyes slid toward Cruz. Were they really expected to put up with this brat?

Her entourage consulted tablets or looked at their feet, but Toby looked at Hunter, and Regina whirled. "I said I wanted the one Queen Elizabeth has."

"Um... Which one is that?" Hunter could name a few dozen models and special editions, but heck. How would he know which model the Queen had?

Clearly, Regina Vanderpelt didn't know either, but she stomped her foot anyway. "The big one."

Cruz twitched his nose. Hunter just shrugged.

"And what's that thing doing next to my car?" Regina shrieked, pointing. "Get it out of there."

The amethyst in her engagement ring flashed in the sun, but Hunter's attention jumped to the big guy on the left —

a personal bodyguard, no doubt — when the man grabbed a broom and lunged into the garage.

Hunter's first worry was that the guy would ding the car, but then he heard a piteous mewing sound and the scramble of tiny paws. He dashed in, body-checked the bodyguard aside, and scooped up a tiny calico kitten before the man could hit it.

"It's just a kitten," he protested, cuddling it to his chest.

"Well, it looks filthy, and I don't want it near my car — even if it isn't the car I wanted," Regina sniffed. "Now, about that ice sculpture, Veronica..." She breezed on, and Hunter and Cruz watched her go.

We are so not taking this job, Cruz murmured into his mind.

Hunter nodded. No way was he working for that spoiled brat.

"Don't fuck with me again," Regina's bodyguard murmured as he shouldered by. He kept his eyes down, though — a sure sign he recognized who was top dog.

Hunter turned, keeping the kitten sheltered while he nuzzled it with his chin. "Poor little guy."

"Calicos are always female," Cruz pointed out.

It figured a tiger would know that.

Hunter petted the kitten gently, imagining the tiny creature's panic and confusion all too well. "Did you lose your mom?" he whispered, holding it close. "Don't worry, I won't let the bad guys get you." He shot a look at Regina Vanderpelt's back. "We'll get you out of here, little one."

I'd love to shift in front of all these people and teach them to pick on someone their own size, Cruz growled into his mind. *You know — show our fangs, snarl a few times. That would do it.*

Hunter was tempted too, and his inner bear doubly so. But he and Cruz knew better than to shift in front of humans — him, most of all. Most shifters relished their ability to change between forms, but he'd had the joy of it pounded out of him at an early age. The distant relatives who had reluctantly taken him in after his mother's death had forbidden him to shift.

That father of yours, they tut-tutted.

His father was half wild grizzly, half shifter, which gave Hunter the rare ability to shift forms as a child rather than starting as a young adult. His mother had seen it as a blessing, but his city-dwelling aunt had considered it a curse.

Never, ever shift where a human can see you. You understand?

Most humans didn't know about the existence of shifters. If they discovered the truth, their fears would spark the kind of frenzied witch-hunts that had nearly annihilated shifters centuries before.

Hide your bear side. No one can know about us.

If only humans understood that there were good and bad shifters just like there were good and bad people.

Never, ever let your bear out. Who knows how wild your inner beast might be?

So he'd done his best to pretend he didn't have a second soul inside. His relatives insisted on it, and he wanted — needed — to please them. He'd done his best to fit in, but all the while, his inner bear had ached and cried.

Please, please let me out. Please. I promise I'll be good.

The suffering went on for years until a kind old owl shifter named Georgia Mae came along and brought him to her foster home on Maui. There, he'd met Kai and Ella, an orphaned fox shifter, and his life changed. Georgia Mae allowed him to shift forms. In fact, she encouraged it, taking her three charges to remote stretches of state park land. Georgia Mae would soar overhead with Kai, keeping Hunter and Ella in sight while they explored in their shifter forms.

Hunter would never forget the feeling of shackles falling from his feet in those early days.

I'm freeee! his bear had hollered, prancing around, trying to sniff everything at once. *I'm free.*

It had taken years, but he'd slowly started internalizing Georgia Mae's words. *You are who you are. And you're wonderful.*

But it had all come crashing down three weeks ago when he'd shifted into bear form to save Dawn. Her look of horror had haunted him ever since and put the shackles back on his soul.

Come on, Cruz rumbled in his mind. *Let's get the hell out of here. I need to shift and claw a few trees after dealing with these people.*

Hunter pursed his lips. He could claw all the trees in West Maui, but that wouldn't help him win his mate. Maybe work would get his mind off the vagaries of fate.

As if working for that little brat will help. Cruz waved a disgusted hand in the direction of Regina Vanderpelt.

Veronica, the personal assistant, hung back for half a second while a ruddy man hurried up to her.

"About the change she wanted to the wedding cake," he asked. "The latest change, I mean."

"Yes?" Veronica sighed.

"Is that the final change?" he asked, pleading with his eyes.

Veronica's lips pinched ever so slightly. "Let's call it final — for now."

"Veronica!" Regina hollered, shoving a man out of her way. He was a big, solid kanaka — a native Hawaiian — yet he went sprawling, and it was all he could do to keep the trolley he had been pushing from toppling over.

"Whoa. The little bitch has some serious power, doesn't she?" Cruz murmured.

Veronica closed her eyes briefly then hurried off after her boss.

Hunter turned inland and sniffed. There it was again. That scent that made the hair on the back of his neck stand up the way lurking danger always did. Still far away, but closing in, or so his imagination wanted to believe. He hugged the kitten closer.

Lorraine from resort security spoke again. "Mr. Bjornvald, Mr. Khala, I'd like you to meet our liaison with the Maui police."

The moment Hunter looked up and spotted the new arrival, his joints locked up. Walking toward him was the most beautiful woman in the world. Dawn's black hair, in its usual braid, shone in the sun, and her dark eyes were as full of mystery as always. Was it really her, or were his dreams growing more vivid every day?

Dawn stopped dead in her tracks, staring at him.

"Hunter," she whispered.

"Dawn," he murmured, enjoying the simple act of saying her name.

Lorraine looked from one to the other. "You know each other? Great. Let me show you where we've based security operations for this event." She set off, but neither Hunter nor Dawn budged.

Cruz cleared his throat. "This is where we make our exit, bro."

Hunter didn't move, but his mind spun. He wanted nothing to do with this extravagant wedding, not even as a hired hand. But if Dawn was here. . .

We can stay and be close to our mate, his inner bear whispered.

He shook his head. Being around Dawn would kill him with reminders of the happy ending he'd never get.

This job will be hell, Cruz grumbled.

The breeze teased Hunter's nostrils with one more hint of trouble brewing somewhere over the horizon.

We have to stay to protect our mate, his bear said.

How real was that danger, though? Especially when staying meant torturing himself all over again — and torturing Dawn, too.

"Are you coming?" Lorraine asked, turning back to them.

Cruz appeared ready to run for the hills. Dawn looked as happy about her assignment as Hunter was, but she held her shoulders straight and stepped forward.

"Coming."

"What about you?" Lorraine asked, gesturing impatiently at Hunter.

Come on, man. Don't do this to yourself, Cruz murmured. *Don't do this to me, either.*

Hunter closed his eyes. Why was life a series of tough choices? His friend versus the woman he couldn't have. His heart versus his mind. Duty versus destiny.

He considered for exactly one second longer before handing the kitten to Cruz. "Take care of the little one for me," he whispered before raising his voice and following Dawn. "Coming."

Chapter Five

By the time Dawn got home that evening, she was exhausted — from the sun, from hours of going over security plans and endless calls, and most of all, from the strain of having to work beside Hunter all day.

His dark, sorrowful eyes made her heart weep. His gravelly voice reached into the depths of her soul and stirred embers she'd thought long extinct. The few times they'd brushed up against each other, a thousand sensual sparks flared through her nerves. But each time, they had skittered apart, and the brief exchanges they'd had were strictly business. If he called her Officer Meli one more time, she'd scream.

Of course, she had only herself to blame, because Hunter had been the reserved gentleman he always was, while she had forced herself to don her toughest mental armor and give him the cold shoulder all day. She had to if she was going to resist the pull that kept drawing her in. Whatever form of black magic gave Hunter the ability to change into a bear must have affected her, too, and she had to resist before it pulled her over to the dark side.

"Long day?" Lily Takeo, her landlord, called from the porch of her tidy cottage set high in the hills.

Dawn nodded. A long day of heat pooling deep in her body and a primal hunger in her bones. Just being around Hunter made her feel like a cat in heat.

The irony made her want to tear her hair out. The only man her body yearned for was a well-concealed beast.

"Long day," she echoed, stepping slowly toward the tiny guest house around the back. Her home. Her escape pod. Her illusionary corner of the universe where she could feel totally in control.

Which was probably part of her problem with Hunter — around him, she always wanted to throw caution to the wind. To feel wild and free.

She frowned. The one time she'd tried wild and free... Suffice it to say, it hadn't ended well.

"Any word from that beau of yours?" Lily asked.

Dawn bit her lip. Up until she'd discovered the truth about Hunter, she'd been slowly trying to work up her nerve to ask him out. She hadn't told Lily about Hunter being a bear because she'd promised not to divulge his secret. And even if she hadn't promised, how would she explain something as impossible as that?

I can't ask out the man I've been crushing on for the past fifteen years. What if he changes into a grizzly again?

Knowing Lily — sweet, kindhearted Lily, who must have been a heck of a flirt in her day — she would completely dismiss that minor detail with a wave her hands. *Such a nice young man.* Dawn could picture Lily leaning in with a naughty smile. *And such big hands. You know what they say about big hands, right?*

Dawn snorted at her own train of thought. What would Lily say about bear paws?

"I told you, Lily. I decided I'm not ready." There. Cheap excuse. That ought to work.

But not with Lily. "Sweetheart, it's time you put the past behind you. Not all men are animals."

Dawn barely held back her reply. *This one is. Literally.*

"A beautiful woman like you..." Lily started.

Dawn crinkled her nose. That was the problem. She attracted men for all the wrong reasons. No one saw her for who she really was.

Except Hunter, said the little voice in the back of her mind.

She picked up her pace, ready to hide away in her own four walls when Lily changed the subject. "I bet you don't feel like cooking tonight."

Dawn let her shoulders slump. No, she didn't.

"Well, you're in luck. You know that cooking class I'm taking?"

No, but it figured. Lily was the busiest widow in the state of Hawaii, it seemed. The woman signed up for every course and every volunteer job on West Maui. Mornings at the animal shelter, weekends at the horticultural society, evenings in the library. Lily was always on the go, always spreading her own brand of Hawaiian sunshine and good cheer.

"I've met the loveliest woman at my cooking class, and she's invited me to dinner — me and a friend. And you're the friend." Lily winked. "She's writing a cookbook and needs us to try out her recipes."

"If she's writing a cookbook, why is she taking a class?"

Lily waved her favorite fan — the one with a Chinese dragon facing off with a tiger. "It's a traditional Hawaiian cooking class, and she's from the mainland. From Nevada, I think. Or was it Arizona?" Lily shrugged. "Some such place where nothing grows. No wonder she moved to Maui. Anyway, she's the best cook in the class. Whatever she makes, it's bound to be delicious."

Dinner did sound tempting, and not just for the meal. Dawn had to get her mind off Hunter and the constant back-and-forth in her mind. Could she trust him? Couldn't she?

"I'll drive," Lily added. "All you have to do is kick back and relax. Now get out of that frumpy uniform and put on something nice."

Dawn stuck her hands on her hips. "Frumpy?" It was her police uniform, and she was proud of it.

"Frumpy." Lily gave a firm nod. "Now, shoo. We leave in fifteen minutes."

It took Dawn more like twenty to shower and change into a strappy pink sundress plus a shrug the color of her eyes and her favorite pair of dressy sandals. The perfect way to turn off her inner cop and just be her — or to try, anyway.

It was dark by the time she stepped into Lily's aging Toyota, and the stars were bright overhead. She leaned back in the passenger seat, angling her head to watch the scenery slip by, breathing in the crisp night air. God, she loved Maui.

37

Lily chatted away about this and that, driving at a ponderous twenty-five miles per hour. Twenty minutes later, she negotiated another curve of the Honoapi'ilani Highway and put the left blinker on to pull onto a dim private road. "Nearly there."

Dawn blinked herself back into focus and slowly sat upright. Wait. What were they doing out here?

Lily hummed as she came to a halt before an imposing gate with a swirling pattern worked into the ironwood.

Dawn's eyes went wide. "Whoa. What are we doing at Koa Point?"

"Going to dinner, sweetheart," Lily purred, reaching out the window to jab at random buttons on the intercom. "Hello?" she bellowed. "Hello?"

Sweat broke out on Dawn's forehead. "Lily—"

"Shush, sweetie. I have to listen to this contraption. Hello? Anyone there? It's me."

Good old Lily, booming like she owned the place while Dawn clutched her seatbelt.

"This can't be right. This is a mistake."

Hunter lived at Koa Point Estate. She couldn't be going to dinner there.

Lily patted her hand. "I'm sure it's the right place."

"Hello, Lily." A woman's voice came over the intercom. "Come on in. We'll meet you at the garage."

We? Dawn wanted to scream. How many shifters lay in wait on the other side of that fence?

The gate slid sideways, and Lily drove in. Dawn looked back and gulped as the gate slid shut behind them. "Lily—"
This place is full of shifters, she wanted to say. *Men who can change into animals at the drop of a dime and rip each other's throats out.*

"Oh, hush, sweetheart. This is going to be great."

Dawn wanted to melt into her seat. Better yet, to slip on the boxing gloves she kept at the gym. But Lily just murmured happily as she looked around.

"My, isn't this nice?"

Well, of course the seaside estate was nice. Dawn had visited the property once, two years earlier, before it changed hands in a multimillion-dollar deal that had most of Maui gossiping for weeks. She knew exactly how nice the place was. But the fact that Hunter lived there...

An owl hooted from the trees. Usually, the sound put her at ease. Tonight, however...

"Lovely," Lily exclaimed at the curving hedges dotted with hibiscus and heliconia.

A willowy figure with red hair pulled into a bun waved to Lily and hugged her the moment she stepped out of the car. "I'm so glad you could make it."

"Dawn," Lily called, looking around. Her voice dropped the second time she called Dawn's name — not quite an order, but close. "Come along, Dawn, and meet my friend Tessa."

Dawn dragged herself out of the car and pasted on a smile. Her eyes darted left and right, the officer in her on high alert.

"So nice to meet you," Tessa said, shaking her hand.

Dawn had seen the woman in passing but had never been introduced. She studied Tessa closely but couldn't find any sign of fur or fangs. But then again, she never would have guessed Hunter was a bear. Was this woman a bear, too? Or maybe a wolf, like Boone?

"Nice to meet you, too."

Tessa led them down a path lit with tiki torches that made shadows flicker and dance. Crickets chirped, and palm fronds swished overhead. All in all, a beautiful, peaceful scene. But Dawn's hand twitched at her hip, and she wished she still had a weapon strapped at her side. Of course, a gun wouldn't help, she remembered a moment later. The attacking wolf Hunter had saved her from hadn't flinched from a bullet at close range. She shivered despite the warm air and held her breath, ready for trouble from any direction.

Hunter saved you. Operative word: saved, the little voice in her mind cried.

Still, she walked along, expecting an ambush at any turn. Night had a way of turning every shadow and sound into danger, and her nerves stretched thin.

Lily, on the other hand, danced along at her usual flowing gait. Her flower-patterned muumuu swung around her body, and she gestured this way and that. "Such lovely bougainvillea. And look at that hibiscus." She broke off a flower and tucked it behind her ear, the picture of island gaiety.

Dawn followed with hunched shoulders and stiff hands, ready to defend herself and Lily. But trouble never came, not even several twists of the path later when Tessa waved toward a beautiful open-sided *hale*, thatched in traditional Hawaiian meeting house style. A line of torches lit the last steps to the open-sided building, and a tall man stepped from the shadows.

Dawn hesitated, but it wasn't Hunter. This man was taller but nowhere near as broad.

"This is Kai," Tessa said. Her whole face lit up as she pressed into his side and patted his chest.

"Hi," he said, reaching out with a friendly handshake. No flash of teeth or clack of hungry fangs. No hungry looks, no red glow to his eyes. Still, Dawn remained on guard.

"Aloha," Lily purred and patted his arm. Then she winked at Tessa as if to say, *I know he's yours, but just let me dream a while, all right?*

Tessa laughed out loud, giving Lily the green light to flirt to her heart's content.

Kai hid a grin and nodded at Dawn. "We know each other from school. Seems like light-years away, huh?"

"Sure does," she murmured. Hunter had grown up not too far from her on the Hana side of Maui — Hunter and a couple of other kids in a foster home run by an eccentric old woman named Georgia Mae. Kai was a year or two older, and a shy girl named Ella had lived there, too. Like Hunter, Kai had certainly filled out since his high school days. Their once-thin chests and arms were now thick with muscle, their torsos extending in a perfect V from the hips. She'd seen Kai around more recently, though she'd never suspected he was a shifter. What kind was he?

"This is Boone," Tessa continued as yet another big, muscled man stepped into the light.

Dawn took a deep breath. Boone had been there the day *it* happened — the day of the fight that had revealed to her what these men really were. Boone had confessed to being a wolf. Cruz, he'd explained, was a tiger. Dawn looked around, thankful Cruz wasn't around.

Lily unfolded her fan with a sassy snap and fluttered her eyelashes. "Why, hello, Boone," she breathed, stretching out the vowels.

"Hi." He grinned.

Lily fanned herself faster.

"I'm Nina." A pretty brunette shook hands with Lily, wearing a smile as genuine and friendly as Dawn had ever seen. Nina had been the one to beg Dawn to give Hunter and the others a chance to explain themselves.

I don't understand it all either, Nina had said that day they'd stood among the carnage of a shifter fight. *But one thing is clear to me, and I know it has to be clear to you. These aren't the bad guys, Officer. Please, let's hear them out.*

Dawn had hesitated, but yes. She had heard them out. But she was still reeling from what they had said.

"We're just waiting for one more person," Tessa said, looking around. "Oh, there you are, Hunter," she said casually as Kai half dragged him out of the shadows with a firm grip.

Dawn's heart thumped. Her knees wobbled. Her fingers flexed. Then she pulled herself to her full five-foot-seven height and forced herself to reply. Damn it, she was Officer Dawn Meli of the Maui police. She was not going to be a victim of her own fears.

"Hello, Hunter," she murmured.

"Oh, you know each other?" Lily exclaimed, looking pleased as punch.

Dawn shot the older woman a suspicious look.

Hunter appeared as shell-shocked as Dawn felt. When he took her hand, his lips shaped her name, but no sound came out. He cleared his throat loudly then turned to Lily with a quiet, "Pleased to meet you."

41

Dawn pursed her lips. For all that Hunter had grown into a big, tough hulk of a man, he still had moments when the shy, gangly kid of the past came through.

Good old Hunter, a little voice in her mind sighed.

She held back an inner snort. If only good old Hunter wasn't a bear.

"Such a nice young man." Lily winked over the edge of her fan.

Dawn pursed her lips. Was she really expected to sit through dinner with him?

Hunter stared at her, and she steeled herself. It was happening again. That mysterious force she'd fought all day started swirling around the two of them, trying to nudge her closer to him. It had taken all her willpower to keep away from Hunter at work, but she was tired now. So, so tired. Her vision grew a little hazy until all she saw was his face and the flickering torches in the background.

Hunter's eyes were dreamy, too, until he jolted and looked down at his feet, breaking the spell.

Dawn rocked back on her heels, blinking at the kitten that had pranced out of the shadows. It wound between Hunter's legs, mewing loudly.

"Whoa there, Keiki," he murmured, scooping it up and rubbing between its ears.

Keiki meant *child.* Lily sighed at the sight of such a big man holding a tiny fur ball, and Dawn nearly did, too.

"Need some milk?" Hunter whispered, carrying the kitten to the kitchen section of the building.

"Be still my heart," Lily murmured, fanning herself in double time.

Dawn exhaled, finding her focus again. God, she hoped she'd be seated across the table from Hunter and not next to him. Otherwise, she might just end the evening in his lap, purring like that kitten.

She looked around, trying to stay on guard. The building was just like the couple of traditional *hale* she'd been in — a huge, open space, except that this one had been furnished with a full kitchen at one side and a living/dining area on the other, complete with couches and what looked like the world's coziest reading nook in one corner. Not a sign of anything unusual, like skulls or trophies of victims as her imagination suggested. It was all perfectly normal — if you were a billionaire, at least.

She glanced over at Hunter, who was kneeling over the kitten by the fridge, then at the other men, and finally in the direction of where the main house stood high on a ridge. The rumor mill had gone wild when Koa Point sold a few years earlier, but no one had definitively identified the new owner.

A very private man, she remembered the newspapers quoting the lawyer who helped seal the multimillion-dollar deal.

She'd never thought much of it before, but now, her mind spun. Was the owner a shifter, too? A sorcerer, perhaps? Was he one of the men here? But she discarded the thought immediately. Whoever the owner was, everyone knew he rarely visited Maui. Hunter and his friends were all Special Forces vets who'd landed the sweetest caretaker's deal in the islands. She turned slowly, wondering where Hunter lived. She spotted a roof poking up among the trees close to the beach, where the surf rolled in. But from what she remembered, Hunter hated open water, so she doubted he'd live close to the beach. Did he live in an apartment above the garage or in another part of the estate?

"Can I get you a drink?" Nina asked, pulling Dawn out of her thoughts. "Wine? Beer?"

"Water, please," Dawn said firmly, folding her napkin into ever smaller, perfectly aligned squares.

She studied the others out of the corner of her eye as dinner got into full swing. But no matter how closely she scrutinized the place or its inhabitants, she couldn't find a hint of anything to fear. On the contrary, it was all so normal. Conversation was lively. The laughter was genuine. Everyone took turns talking and listening without anyone dominating the scene — except Lily, who cracked jokes and flirted outrageously with the men.

"Oh my goodness. This is so good." Lily smacked her lips after a few bites. "The food, I mean. Not the view." She winked at Boone.

Dawn had just worked back the taro leaf wrapped around her pork and snapper, and the first bite just about melted in her mouth.

Kai groaned out loud, and Boone licked his fingers. "Seriously, Tessa. You've outdone yourself."

Tessa grinned. "You guys will eat anything, but I'm glad our guests like it."

Dawn had to agree. "It's amazing."

"Tastes like *laulau* but different," Lily said.

"I steamed it then threw it on the grill for a few minutes. Not too bad, huh?"

Dawn kept looking around, trying to spot a hint of evil or a shadow of black magic, but there didn't seem to be any. Maybe these shifters were really just... normal people, or as close as shifters could be. They were all friendly. Warm. Sincere.

"Boone tried grilling once," Kai started, poking fun at his friend.

"Yeah. Once," Boone laughed.

"Ha. My sister and I wanted to surprise my dad one time..." Laughter shone in Tessa's eyes as she related a tale of a Father's Day gone wrong.

"Sundays were always pancake day for me and my mom," Nina added with a wistful smile.

"I think pancake Sundays are just what we need here at Koa Point," Boone murmured, taking her hand.

Koa, Dawn thought. The Hawaiian word for the toughest kind of wood was also the word for an elite class of warrior. That fit Hunter, Kai, and Boone perfectly, but each had a softer, gentler side, too.

"This is amazing," Kai said, raising his glass to Tessa.

His voice was full of affection, and Dawn could see Tessa glow. Their love was as obvious as the shine in Boone's eyes when he looked at Nina.

You could have that, too, the little voice in her mind said. *Love. Respect. Affection. Trust.*

She peeked at Hunter. If there was one man she'd ever been tempted to trust, it was him. But he'd already made one startling revelation. What other secrets might he be hiding from her?

Hunter's mocha eyes met hers with an expression so wistful, she nearly reached for his hand. The candle set between them flickered with a warm, yellow glow. Somewhere in the distance, surf rolled over the sand, and a faint breeze made the thatching whisper overhead. Really whispering, as if talking to her.

Him. Hunter. He's the one.

The crickets chirping outside took up the same call, and the birds rustling in the bushes did, too. As if all of Mother Nature wanted her to understand one simple thing.

This is a good man. You can trust him. He is the one.

She tried pushing the thought away, because that could be the voice of some dark, brooding force trying to trick her into a false sense of security.

A breath of wind nearly extinguished the candle, but then the tiny flame stood tall and bright again, holding back the darkness of night.

Dawn stared over the flame, gazing deep into Hunter's eyes. Damn it, it was so hard to stay on guard around a man who exuded *I-will-cherish-you-forever* vibes. She had a sixth sense for trouble, but all her internal alarms were silent. How could Hunter be guided by evil if he only made her feel good?

The dinner guests at the table may as well have wandered off for all Dawn noticed. She sat, deaf and mute to the others. But inside, her body heated and sang.

Hunter. He's the one.

Hunter's long, dark lashes barely moved, he was so intent on her. Dawn felt light-headed, staring into his eyes. Intoxicated. Fascinated, the way the most sensual hula performances fascinated her. The kind performed on a beach at night with swaying hips, bare bellies, and *pahu* drums beating a frenzied beat.

Maybe he really was the one. Maybe she could trust him, after all.

"Dawn," someone called, but the sound was faint, as if spoken at the end of a long tunnel. "Dawn."

Dawn cleared her throat sharply, breaking away from Hunter's steady gaze. "What was the question?" She reached for her water glass and took a huge gulp.

"I said, tell us about this celebrity wedding," Lily prodded.

"Well..." Dawn and Hunter started at the same time.

Lily clapped. "Oh, you're working together? How nice!"

Funny how Lily didn't appear the least bit surprised. Dawn was going to have a long talk with her on the way home.

Everyone else looked on expectantly. Hunter studied his fork. Dawn cleared her throat — again.

"Is that Regina Vanderwhatshername as bad as they say?" Lily asked.

Everyone leaned forward for the juicy details as Dawn fished for words.

"I guess a lot of brides get stressed," she managed. There. That sounded diplomatic, right?

Kai snorted. "There's stressed, and there's spoiled brat. I took her photographer up for some aerial shots today, and she just about smacked the camera out of his hands when he showed her the results. She made him go up again saying — and I quote — 'Make sure it doesn't look so windy this time.'"

"I'm glad I decided not to take a job with the catering company, after all," Tessa said. "What did you think of her, Hunter?"

The kitten had jumped into his lap, and he petted it while he mulled over a reply. "I guess I didn't notice anything much."

Dawn raised her eyebrows, admiring his restraint. Where was the raging animal she had seen a few weeks ago? When the wolf had attacked her, Hunter had turned into a marauding beast. Did animal outrage come out of nowhere and take over his body from time to time?

An owl hooted, and everyone quieted, listening to the muted call.

"*Pu'eo*," Lily whispered.

Nina tilted her head.

"*Pu'eo* means owl," Dawn explained.

"Where is it?" Tessa asked, craning her neck.

Kai pointed one way, but Dawn pointed overhead. "Listen. He's about to fly over the roof."

Everyone's heads followed the sound of wing flaps overhead.

"Wow. How did you know what it was going to do?" Nina asked.

Dawn shrugged. Some things, she just sensed. If only she could read shifters the way she could read birds.

"*Pu'eo* is Dawn's *aumakua*," Lily said.

Nina cocked her head. "Auma-what?"

Dawn looked at Lily. *Aumakua* were hard to explain, especially to someone who didn't grow up on the islands.

"Ancestral spirit," Hunter surprised her by whispering. "Like a family god."

"The owl is a protector," Lily said.

Hunter's eyes flashed at Dawn, communicating something that looked like, *I will protect you.*

He had. He'd saved her. Twice now. Once way back in high school, from an ugly incident she'd disciplined herself not to think about, and again a few weeks ago, when the wolf had come within a hair of her throat.

"Do you have an *aumakua*, Lily?" Tessa asked.

"Sure. Most everyone with roots in the islands does. Mine is the *pua'a* — the stubborn old pig." She chuckled. "Lucky Dawn. I swear she has the night vision of an owl."

Dawn kept her lips sealed. It was true, but it didn't seem like much compared to her hosts. They could transform into animals, for goodness' sake!

"What other *aumakua* are there?" Tessa asked.

"Oh, there are lots. Bats. Sharks. Dragons..."

"Dragons?" Tessa's eyes went wide.

"Sure." Lily fanned herself casually. "You can even see them from time to time."

Tessa choked on her food. "You can?"

Kai nodded. "There's one over on Molokai."

Lily shook her head. "That's just a shape nature carved into the rocks. There are real dragons, too. *Mo'o*, we call them. I've seen them flying over West Maui at night."

Kai was the one choking now. Tessa's eyes glowed green, the color of the pendant around her neck.

"Yes, indeed," Lily went on, cheery as can be. "There are a couple of them around."

Dawn's eyes went wide as she looked at Tessa and Kai. Could it really be?

"But don't worry," Lily finished with a sly smile. "They seem like nice dragons to me."

Chapter Six

"Lily," Dawn admonished the older woman after dinner wound down and the two of them walked the path back toward the car. "Why on earth would you say such a thing?"

"Which thing, sweetheart? Oh, you mean the comment about Kai's biceps? You didn't think they were nice?"

Dawn shook her head. Lily had had a hell of a time that evening, play-flirting and making the men blush with her open ogling of chests and thick arms. But that wasn't what Dawn was referring to. "I mean the thing about dragons."

Lily fluttered her eyelashes innocently. "What about them?"

Dawn sighed and took a step back. There was no reasoning with that woman — especially now that Tessa was coming up from behind.

"Thank you so much for coming out here tonight," Tessa said.

"Oh, I had a wonderful time." Lily beamed. "Didn't you, Dawn?"

She nodded. "Dinner was great. Thank you."

She meant it, too. Dragons, bears, and wolves aside, Dawn had to admit that the evening was nothing like she had feared. The Pacific was serving up one of those gorgeous, starlit nights when everything seemed peaceful and serene. The food was divine, and the company was nice. Really nice. Who'd have thought dinner with a group of shapeshifters could be such a pleasant event?

And, damn. What did it say about her social life that her best night out in the past couple of years was one spent with a flirty seventy-year-old and a group of people who each hid a wild, animal side?

The fears that had accelerated her heart rate on the way in had all but dissipated, though she still wasn't sure what to make of Hunter and his friends. But never mind — she'd survived the night. It was getting late, and she had work in the morning. Another day at the Kapa'akea resort, which had its pluses and minuses. The plus was seeing Hunter again. The minus was... well, seeing Hunter again. The man made part of her want to shred her own self-control and toss it to the wind.

They were nearly at the car when Lily threw up her hands in dismay. "Oh, my purse! Sweetheart, can you fetch it for me?"

Dawn turned and headed back down the path, running her hands over the awapuhi growing on either side. It was dark, but she could make out every curved petal of the ginger flower. They interlocked, one nestled inside the other, each petal arching back to the night sky. Dawn tipped her chin up to study the stars. Canis Major was high in the sky, and Sirius, the Dog Star, shone bright. Then came Gemini and then... Her step faltered. That was the Great Bear. Guardian of the night sky or a hunter in disguise?

She was so engrossed in thought that she nearly walked into a tree. "Oops."

Except it wasn't a tree. It was Hunter. He grunted and steadied her before quickly letting go.

"Sorry," he murmured, stepping back quickly.

"Sorry," she gulped, thinking how strange it was that he was so flighty around her. She ought to be the flighty one, right?

Then it hit her. All this time, she'd been worried about Hunter hurting her when it had been her, hurting him. Poor Hunter — as big and mighty as he was, part of him was still the lonely kid who'd never really fit in. And for the past weeks, she'd been as cold and standoffish as the kids at school had been when Hunter was the new kid on the block. She hung her head a little. Hunter had only ever been sweet to her. Why couldn't she bring herself to trust him?

He held something out, extending his arm so she wouldn't have to come too close. "Lily forgot this."

Dawn took a deep breath. She could just take the purse and go, but how could she ignore that pained look in his eyes?

"Hunter," she whispered, ignoring the purse and slowly reaching for his arm. It was thick as a tree branch yet surprisingly soft with tiny curls of hair. She moved her hand up and down slightly, in part admiring his bulk, in part wondering what it might feel like to touch bear fur.

He didn't say anything, and he didn't move, though his nostrils flared.

Hers did, too, because damn. He smelled so good. Like Maui. Like koa, the toughest kind of wood.

"I'm sorry I've been so...so..." She fished for words. Cruel? Mean? Cold? "Distant," she decided. "I just..."

"Not your fault," he murmured.

She looked at him. It wasn't exactly his fault, either. If he hadn't stopped the wolf that had attacked her, she would be dead.

"You saved me. Again." Maybe it didn't matter that he'd done so in bear form. Either way, he'd put himself on the line to defend her.

You can judge a man by his actions, not his words, Lily had once said.

Hunter waved a hand as if it were nothing.

"It's just that I never suspected..." Her words petered away. What exactly was she trying to say?

"No problem. I get it," he said, giving her an easy out. All she had to do was take Lily's purse, thank him, and walk away with a confident stride. He'd get the message and leave her alone once and for all.

Except she didn't want him to leave her alone. Not in her heart, not in her soul. So instead of turning, she slid her hand higher, past his elbow and all the way to his shoulder. Trying to reconcile herself to the idea that the beast might be as much of a gentle giant as the man.

Her heart revved, though, and her fingers shook a tiny bit.

Hunter's brown eyes shone in the dark, but he didn't flinch.

"I don't get it," she whispered, inching closer. "Why is it that around you, I can't seem to think straight?"

The left side of his mouth crooked up. "Around you, I could never see straight."

Her right foot stepped forward, and her left followed without her even realizing it, and suddenly, she was sharing his personal space. Easing into it the way she might ease into a warm bath.

Her blood prickled and danced in her veins. Her breath came in jittery, uneven waves. Was she really standing that close to Hunter?

A second later, her eyes went wide. Because she wasn't just standing close to Hunter. She was kissing him. Gingerly. Softly. Reaching with her lips. Her hands reached, too, slipping around his neck as if they'd kissed a hundred times when, in fact, she'd only ever done it once in real life.

But kissing Hunter — a bear shifter... Was she crazy?

Maybe she was because, wow — she was enjoying it. The soft, smooth feel of his lips. The hint of something powerful slumbering inside him, kept carefully leashed. She pressed close enough to feel the beat of his heart. A low, steady beat that represented Hunter perfectly. Solid yet fragile. Quiet, yet powerful. His lips barely moved over hers, but her soul danced.

God, this feels so good, she wanted to sigh.

She slid her arms behind his shoulders — well, she tried, given their breadth — and leaned deeper into the kiss. An unrushed, skipping-through-fields-of-flowers kiss. The feeling of coming home after a long, long time away.

If Hunter's grip had been a little tighter or his lips more demanding, she might have pushed him away. But his touch was so gentle that all she wanted was more. More than she'd ever let herself dare to desire.

"Dawn..." Hunter murmured.

She hummed because it felt so good to hear him say her name. *Officer Meli* was for strangers. Hunter was a friend.

"Dawn..." he whispered, gently pulling back.

She might have kept her hands fisted in his shirt and her lips glued to his forever if it wasn't for the fluttering of a bird overhead. She took in a sharp breath and stared. Did he not want what she wanted?

The look in Hunter's eyes said he wanted her just as desperately as she wanted him, but, as always, something held him back. He smoothed his hands over her shoulders then pulled her in for a hug. A long, tight hug, the way you hugged someone you'd missed for years.

"Dawn," he whispered, resting his head against hers.

She took a deep breath, inhaling his musky scent, and clutched his shirt. Damn — she'd totally lost control for a minute. Maybe she was the one with an animal side.

"God, Hunter. Remember that kiss under the waterfall?"

She'd been sixteen, he'd been seventeen, and they were the last two kids at the local swimming hole. Splashing and playing had somehow turned to touching and hugging, and when they'd kissed, she thought she'd seen heaven.

He nodded. "That kiss got me through... well, a lot of rough spots."

She ran her hand over a scar on his forearm, wondering what terrible things he might have seen or done all those years he'd spent in far less peaceful places than Maui.

She closed her eyes, remembering the kiss down to the tiniest detail. The flavor of his lips. The slide of his hands over her ribs. The way they fit like they were made for each other. They'd broken apart and gazed into each other's eyes for what seemed like hours until the bushes rustled with a new group of visitors that made them skitter apart.

"Why did you stop seeing me?" she asked. They had vowed to meet back the next day, but Hunter hadn't shown.

His eyes dropped, and he kicked the ground.

"What?" She grasped his arm.

"Your dad. Your dad found out. He came around to my foster mother that night and made a big stink."

She pulled back, gaping. "My dad?"

Hunter nodded. "He said if I ever got within a yard of you, he'd have my ass arrested."

Dawn shook her head. Her dad had been a wisp of a man, and even at seventeen, Hunter had been a big kid. But then again, her father was the district attorney, and she could picture how easily he could threaten someone like Hunter — a kid who had no one to stick up for him except the eccentric old woman who took care of him.

She rested her head on his shoulder and rolled it from side to side. Her dad had been the one to encourage her to date the captain of the football team, Clive, who'd—

She tore her thoughts away from Clive, as she always did. And as for her father... Some judge of character he turned out to be.

"My dad was an ass."

Hunter's chest rose and fell, but he didn't say anything.

I missed you, she wanted to say. *I missed you so much for so many years. And I thought I was finally ready to get closer, but then...*

Then she'd been completely freaked out by him turning into a bear. Dawn stared at her feet.

"Dawn! Are you coming?" Lily's voice boomed out through the night.

She let out a long, uneven breath and backed away slowly, pulling the purse from his hand. "I'd better get going."

Hunter nodded quietly, though his Adam's apple bobbed. Was that hope or rejection in his eyes?

Dawn turned on her heel and did her best not to rush away, feeling his eyes on her the entire time.

"See you soon?" she murmured, unable to resist looking back.

His smile was forced, his hands shoved deep into his pockets. "See you soon."

She wanted to boomerang back into his arms, but she made herself walk on. A minute later, she was in Lily's car and out the estate gate, ordering herself not to look back.

"Lovely people," Lily said as she pulled onto the highway.

Except they're not people, Dawn wanted to say. But, heck. Hunter had such soul and so much sorrow. It wasn't fair to think of him as less than human.

"That Hunter is such a nice man," Lily said, opening the door to a conversation Dawn didn't want to have.

She hummed something neutral and looked at the stars.

"A very attractive man, too." Lily winked.

Like Dawn needed to be told. Even back in high school, he was a sight to behold. But now, there was a wounded warrior appeal to him that made him that much harder to resist.

"So what's the problem, sweetie? You two spent the whole evening gazing into each other's eyes."

"We did not!"

Lily snorted. "I know love when I see it. What's holding you back?"

Dawn picked at a thread in the hem of her shrug. How much could she say? How could she possibly explain?

"There's something inside him that scares me," she said at last, choosing her words carefully.

Lily tut-tutted. "You're not afraid of him. You're afraid of falling in love."

Dawn's eyes went wide, and she snapped her head around. "Why would I be afraid of that?"

"You tell me."

Dawn huffed. Lily could be impossible sometimes.

Still, her mind swirled with answers she couldn't quite bring herself to utter aloud. *Because love makes you vulnerable.* That was one good reason. *Because not every man loves his woman.* There. Another good reason.

And then, of course, there was, *Because I'm afraid I might not be able to love him back.*

Dawn closed her eyes, putting a wall up against the ugly memories in the far reaches of her mind.

Lily tapped her fingers on the steering wheel. "What you need is someone to shake you out of that carefully controlled cage you live in."

"It's not a cage."

"Everything worth having comes with a risk," Lily said. "But without love, you don't really live. Did I tell you about Stanley?"

Dawn watched the scrub blur by at the edge of the road. Lily had shared so many stories about her late husband, Dawn figured she knew them all by heart.

55

"I nearly gave him up," Lily said in an uncharacteristically quiet voice. "I was so young, so foolish, thinking another good man would come along. So I let him go when things started feeling a little too...ordinary. I thought I wanted my freedom. I wanted a more exciting man." Lily sighed. "I found out how empty my life was without him. How no other man could take his place in my heart. Lucky for me, Stanley waited. The man had such faith in true love..."

Dawn's eyes grew misty. Hunter had that unshakeable faith, too. He had faith in her, even when she'd shown so little in him.

"When I think that I could have lost him forever... But I was lucky. We had our second chance, and we used it, honey." Her voice took on a naughty hint again. "Boy, did we use it." She slapped Dawn's thigh, making her jump. "I don't want to see you let your chance slip away."

Dawn closed her eyes. She didn't want that either. But deep inside, her heart was scarred and fragile. Did she really dare?

Lily drove the next few curves in silence then murmured, "A beautiful night, don't you think?"

The sky was perfectly clear, and starlight glittered over the sea. The lush, earthy scent of Maui seemed doubly rich at night, when colors drained away and the landscape slumbered. Dawn breathed deeply and thought back to Hunter's kiss.

She nodded. A beautiful night, indeed.

Chapter Seven

"I still don't get why I wasn't invited to dinner," Cruz grumbled the next morning.

Hunter stirred his oatmeal without saying a word. It was seven a.m. — a ridiculously early hour for a bear shifter to be up, and yet, for the first time in weeks, he felt ready to face a new day. Optimistic, almost. Which was dangerous — he shouldn't get his hopes up about Dawn.

"You weren't invited because you'd scare our guests," Kai told Cruz.

Hunter had the feeling nothing could scare Lily. And though he knew Dawn didn't scare easily, she would have been that much more tense if yet another shifter had been around.

Keiki, the calico kitten, had jumped up onto the table, and he gently pushed her to the side. She made a beeline for Cruz, who scooped her up and nuzzled her with his chin.

"At least someone appreciates me," he muttered.

Hunter hid a grin. Cruz was nowhere near as hard and cold as he pretended to be.

"I wasn't invited either," Silas growled over his coffee.

Tessa snorted. "Because you're scary, Silas, all right? We wanted to make a good impression on Dawn. I mean — on our guests."

Hunter took a sip of coffee. So it had been a setup.

"I am not scary," Silas insisted. His eyes glowed red, and his face drew into a deep scowl.

Tessa rolled her eyes. "Sure. Not scary. Just a little intense."

Nina poured him a coffee, and Silas sighed. He snapped the newspaper open and turned his ire on the politics and natural disasters of the world. A minute later, he just about spat out his coffee. "Look at this."

Hunter leaned closer, as did the others, following Silas's finger to an article on the back page.

Cruz snorted at the picture of Regina Vanderpelt. "We know the little brat is getting married."

Silas pointed to the sidebar of the piece. "No, this part." He started reading from the sidebar. "A security detail will accompany the delivery of Miss Vanderpelt's diamond wedding ring at an undisclosed time..."

"Look at the size of that thing," Tessa murmured.

"Thirty carats, with a value of..." Kai trailed off with a whistle.

Hunter narrowed his eyes on the grainy photo of Regina modeling the ring at a fancy New York jeweler's. "Is it just an ordinary diamond or..."

"That's the question," Silas said. "What if it's a Spirit Stone?"

Everyone went silent except Keiki, who purred in Cruz's arms.

"Could be any diamond." Hunter kept his voice even, but his fingers tightened around his spoon.

Most humans were unaware of the existence of Spirit Stones, but shifters — especially dragons — coveted the jewels for their supernatural powers. Another one of the stones showing up on Maui was trouble, guaranteed.

Silas looked from Tessa to Nina. "We know the stones call to each other, and now that two have awakened..."

Tessa had arrived on Maui a few months ago and inadvertently set off a battle for an emerald known as the Lifestone. Nina had nearly been killed when shifter mercenaries attempted to kidnap her — along with the Firestone she'd inherited.

Hunter put his spoon down. Shit, all he needed was a few dragons to swoop down over Maui in search of a Spirit Stone. That would scare Dawn off for good.

"Which of the Spirit Stones is the diamond?" Tessa asked.

"The Windstone," Silas murmured into the depths of his mug.

"We can't be sure it's a Spirit Stone," Kai tried.

"No, we can't," Silas agreed. He pointed at Hunter then at Cruz. "But you two are going to keep your eyes open and tell me the second you can confirm if that diamond is anything other than a fancy stone. You, too, Kai."

Cruz groaned. "I have a better idea. You go deal with Regina and her entourage. Keiki and I will hold down the fort here."

Silas shook his head and stood quickly. "I need to get in touch with some contacts and find out more about that diamond."

"I'll watch Keiki," Tessa offered.

"Great. Thanks." Cruz scowled until he caught Kai's growl. A growl of warning that said, *You watch how you talk to my mate.*

Cruz sighed and handed the kitten to Tessa. "Sorry. Here. I mean, thanks."

Cruz muttered all the way to the resort, though Hunter barely noticed. His mind was on Dawn and the complication the diamond posed. Danger seemed to accompany those Spirit Stones wherever they appeared.

His hands were tight around the wheel, his brow heavy with concern. The security guards at the gate skittered out of the way and hastily waved him through. But the second he parked the Jeep at the resort and spotted Dawn, his mind went blissfully blank. Her silky black hair hung over the white shirt of her police uniform, and her barely concealed curves teased him.

Mate, his bear hummed happily. *There's our mate.*

"Good morning," he managed once he regained enough motor control to lumber over her way.

Two plain, ordinary words when what he really wanted to do was run over, hug her, and spin around a few times. His heart leaped every time he saw Dawn, and his world brightened the way some people felt when they first stepped foot on Maui — breathing the fragrant air, tipping their chins up to the sun, smiling from the beauty of it all. Today more than ever because maybe, just maybe, she'd slowly come around. She'd kissed him the previous night, and his inner bear was still giddy about it.

She loves me! She loves me!

"Morning," Dawn replied, cool as a cucumber except for the tiny quiver in her lip.

His mouth moved, too, because there was so much more he wanted to say. To ask. To explain. But he forced himself to take a deep breath and get back to work without further ado. One kiss might not mean that much to her, even if it meant the world to him.

"Beautiful day," she murmured, walking at his side.

It is now that you're here, he wanted to say.

No staring at her, no matter how beautiful she is, he ordered his bear. *No growling at other men. No bared teeth.*

In other words, pretend I don't exist? his bear mourned.

All the ghosts of his past reared up at once, moaning and rattling their chains. As a child, he'd been told to bury his inner bear and never, ever let the beast free. It had taken years to work himself free of those scars. Now, he was right back where he'd started — denying his bear side.

And God, did that feeling cut to the bone. But even so, his bear suffered in silence. She was worth it.

"Beautiful day," he murmured.

"I wanted to go over the arrangements for—" Dawn started when a screech sounded in the distance.

Everyone winced and turned their heads.

"Coming, Regina," Veronica, the personal assistant, said, hurrying out the front door of the hotel.

"Ah, the bride is up and raring to go," Dawn muttered.

Cruz shook his head and shot Hunter a private remark. *I can't believe Silas forced me to come back here. Don't you think he's grasping at straws?*

Hard to tell. Hunter sniffed the air, searching for trouble or the faint scent of shifter he'd caught the day before. But the dewy morning air didn't reveal much, so he followed Dawn into the room set up as security headquarters.

"Why, hello, honey," the asshole at the door purred at Dawn. A towering, barrel-chested guy — the type who'd served a year or two in the Marines then spent the next thirty years hiring out to security firms. His eyes roved over Dawn.

A good thing Cruz was there to keep Hunter from flinging that asshole against the nearest wall. Instead, he growled, and the man shrank back.

Dawn's eyes flashed at both of them. *Call me Officer Meli,* they blazed at the asshole, and *I can handle this myself* to Hunter.

"I beg your pardon?" she demanded, not the least fazed.

"I mean, good morning, Officer."

Dawn sniffed and walked on while Hunter pinned the man with a killer glare. *Check out her ass, and I will teach you a lesson you'll never forget.*

The man cleared his throat, hastily tidied some papers, and rapped his knuckles on the table. "All right, people. Settle down." He thumped a big hand on his own chest, introducing himself. "Ken Thomas of Armor Security."

Hunter heaved an inner sigh. It figured this guy would be head of security.

Cruz rolled his eyes. *We have to work with this arrogant ass?*

Hunter shrugged. *No problem. We'll do the usual.*

Cruz grinned back. *The usual* meant quickly establishing alpha superiority and then doing their jobs as they saw fit. Any fool could call himself the head of security. Hunter and Cruz were the warriors who got the job done.

The morning briefing covered all the usual things — ID checks at the main entrances, patrols of the fenced grounds, and details of possible weak points.

"The weather report forecasts a massive swell set to hit Maui in a few days," the head of security said.

"God, no," someone groaned. "We'll never hear the end of it if the little bitch — I mean, Miss Vanderpelt — doesn't get the sunny beach wedding of her dreams."

"You mean no one passed her orders on to Mother Nature?" another man cracked.

Hunter glanced out the window to the bustling resort grounds, sensing a different kind of storm building.

Ken Thomas went on with his brief. "The storm won't reach us, but the swell might. And if it does, that complicates things."

"Complicates, how?" someone asked.

"Thirty-foot waves kind of complicated," he replied. "But that's more a matter for the wedding planners than security. On the plus side, surf like that will help keep anyone from trying to sneak in from the beach side. Our main concern is the press. The reporters are already all over this event, and they'll do anything to get pictures of this circus."

Hunter winced at the thought of exploding flashes and shouted questions. A damn good thing he wasn't a celebrity.

"There's also the possibility of sabotage," the security chief went on. "The Vanderpelt oil business has created its share of enemies."

Hunter wrinkled his nose, wondering if the Vanderpelts had a hand in the Alaskan pipeline that had forced him from home. His mother had steadfastly refused to give in to pressure to sell, and one day, a gang had torched his home. She'd died defending it — and defending Hunter, who'd been too young to fight. He closed his eyes and clenched his fists, reminding himself it was all so long ago.

"What about the diamond?" Dawn asked.

Hunter's eyes snapped open. Dawn knew about the diamond?

When she caught his surprised look, she rolled her eyes, and he cursed himself. Of course, Dawn knew. The diamond had been in the news, and the police would have been informed, too.

"We will be briefing everyone about delivery arrangements when the time comes," Ken Thomas said.

"This wedding is already putting a strain on police resources. Refusing to inform us of the delivery date makes it difficult to provide the level of protection required," she said, staring down the head of security, a man twice her size.

"We will be briefing everyone at the appropriate time," he repeated in a monotone.

Dawn ground her teeth, and Hunter did his best to glare at the man without bristling too obviously. Dawn could hold her own, and he had to respect that. But shit, it was hard when all he wanted to do was stalk over to the bastard and shake him until his silver fillings came loose.

A phone rang, giving the asshole an easy out. He snapped his fingers. "To work, everybody."

Hunter filed out the door with everyone else, jostling shoulders with Cruz until they parted ways on the porch. Cruz veered off to the left to check the perimeter of the huge property — a task that suited the reclusive tiger perfectly. Hunter, meanwhile, covered the main grounds.

"What do you think?" Dawn asked, looking over the beehive of activity on the lawn.

His bear sighed. *I think I can't live without you.*

He forced his mind into work mode and waved at the truck grinding down the delivery road. "It's damn near impossible to check every supplier in an event of this size. There are too many cracks to guarantee no one slips through."

She nodded. "And too little information. Too little planning ahead. I don't like it one bit. Like the diamond ring. The secrecy around it is ridiculous. I have to wonder how the woman is ever going to wear the thing if it's so damn valuable."

Hunter frowned. If only Dawn knew how valuable that diamond might be. More valuable than any human might suspect. And, shit. Wasn't that important information for the police liaison to have? He scuffed the ground. God, did he feel low and dirty, keeping secrets from Dawn.

He was about to murmur some response when the breeze carried a new scent to him, and his head snapped to the right. The scent of shifter — a shifter he didn't know.

He sniffed deeply then caught himself. If Dawn caught him acting like a wild animal, she'd flip.

"Sorry, I have to check on the construction crew over there," he said, turning away so she couldn't see his nostrils flaring on the wind.

"I have to oversee the main entrance," she sighed.

When she stepped away, Hunter felt pulled in two directions. His heart wanted to follow Dawn, but his nose ordered him to explore that unknown scent. So he forced himself away from her and set off, following his nose.

That was a shifter, for sure, and it was nearby. A canine of some kind, but not a wolf. A fox? He stared at one face after another as caterers, construction workers, and florists hustled around, all intent on their work. Then he followed his keen nose to the raised platform where a crew was setting up speakers and wires for a band. He ticked one human after another off his mental list until his eyes narrowed on a stooped man who cracked a joke and cackled loudly. That was him — the shifter. The intruder. Hunter's claws pressed against his fingernails, eager to burst out.

The man froze and turned slowly then locked eyes with Hunter. His mouth tightened, and his eyes hit the ground in a sign of submission. A moment later, he faked a casual smile. "Heya."

Heya, my ass, Hunter wanted to say. He jerked his head to the side, ordering the shifter to step toward the trees where they would be out of earshot of the humans. Hunter followed, cracking his knuckles, trying to place the scent. Stooped shoulders. Cackling laugh. A strangely elongated neck. What the hell kind of shifter was that?

It hit him a moment later. Hyena. What the hell was a hyena doing on Maui?

He resisted the urge to throw the smaller man against a tree trunk, crossing his arms instead. "Show me your ID. Now."

The man grinned and held out a photo ID that said Rupert Hayes. "Hey, man. Don't get all worked up."

Hunter glowered. Maui was his turf. He'd get worked up if he wanted, especially with a wheedling hyena like this.

"What are you doing here?"

"I'm with the band, man. Just trying to earn an honest living, like you." The word *honest* slid off his tongue far too smoothly.

Hunter sniffed for the telltale hint of a lie, but the hyena was good at masking his emotions.

"Listen," the hyena said. "I swear, I'm not here to make trouble. You can check me out with the company."

Hunter fully intended to, but he still wasn't satisfied. On the other hand, he couldn't exactly toss a man off the premises with no firm grounds.

"I will," he growled. "And I'll be watching you."

The man shrank back when Hunter squared his shoulders. Then he rattled out another cackling laugh and sidestepped, making his way back to work. "It's always good to be vigilant, but believe me, I'm just here to work. And then I'll be on my way to the next job, and the next. You know how it goes." He scurried away.

Hunter growled, watching the man go until a shrill voice made him wince.

"That's all wrong!" Regina cried.

Hunter turned to see the bride gesturing at the ice sculpture. The gesture nearly launched the pink straw and tiny umbrella out of her coconut shell cocktail glass.

"You want a what?" The sculptor blanched.

Hunter ignored them, turning back to the hyena. But the crafty creature had already slipped out of sight. Hunter scanned the foliage, then the crowd.

"You heard me." Regina stamped her foot at the sculptor, and Hunter swore the ground shook a little bit. "I want a swan. To match the cake. Wait — did we get the cake fixed?" She turned to Veronica.

Hunter caught a glimpse of the hyena shifter disappearing into the delivery truck. Whoever that shifter was, Hunter would keep his eye on the beast.

"The last change to the cake was back to bride and groom figures," Veronica said as Hunter edged by.

Regina turned red. "No! Not a bride and groom. I want a swan! And the ice sculpture has to match."

Veronica tapped into her device. "No problem."

The sculptor's look said, *Big problem,* but he kept his lips sealed.

Luckily, that wasn't an issue Hunter had to resolve. And anyway, he had enough on his hands. He sighed and counted the mounting issues. A diamond that might or might not be a Spirit Stone. A woman he couldn't get his mind off. An unknown shifter who might or might not be plotting something.

And if so, what?

Hunter shook his head. Wherever this Rupert guy came from, he was a complication Hunter really didn't need.

Chapter Eight

Dawn stood high on a rocky point over the resort, sweeping it with her eyes. Looking for danger, it might seem like, when in reality she was looking for Hunter.

It was their third day on the job and their third day of tangoing gingerly around each other. No matter how hard she tried to focus on work and pretend Hunter was just another man, she couldn't convince herself of the lie. The bear shifter part almost stopped feeling significant, because the man was so damn... sweet. He always seemed to amble along and pass her a bottle of water when the sun was at its highest — and then he'd quietly back away. He would turn up out of nowhere when one of the bride's entourage was at their pissiest to announce that Dawn was needed — immediately! — somewhere else. Ken Thomas, the head of Armor Security, was a little awed by Hunter, and every time he paused to ask Hunter's opinion, Hunter would clear his throat and turn the question over to Dawn with a respectful, "Officer Meli, what do you think?" Then he'd tilt his head to listen — really listen — and the others did, too.

He had a knack for heading the same way as she at exactly the same time, when he would adjust his pace and merge paths with her with a quiet, undemanding "Hi."

One syllable. Two letters. But they sent a hot rush through her body every time.

How a man that big could come off as so sweet, she had no idea. But he was. Sweet — and sexy as hell. The way he ran his fingers through his hair made her fantasize about those fingers parting her hair, and when he walked beside her, she had the overwhelming urge to brush up against his shoulder, just to feel his heat. The way he rubbed his neatly trimmed beard made her imagine him touching her skin with the same slow, ponderous strokes. Her fantasies grew more and more detailed until she imagined him inching closer and kissing her bare skin on a moonlit night.

She puffed a breath of air upward over her face, trying to cool off.

It was as if Hunter had found a mesmerizing new cologne and doubled the dose every day, because she couldn't stop daydreaming about him — make that, dreaming about him and her naked and indulging in reckless fantasies in a dozen hidden corners of the resort.

At the same time, Hunter kept his distance, taking such care not to crowd her that she almost wished he would, just to give her something to resent.

Without love, you don't live. Lily's words kept echoing through her mind, making it impossible to focus on the job.

So she'd come up to the rocky outcrop in an attempt to clear her head. Surf pounded the shoreline below, making the water churn the way her emotions roiled inside her.

Get your shit together, Officer Meli, she ordered herself. *All you did was kiss him.*

But it was more than a kiss, and she knew it. It was the step over an invisible threshold her soul had dreamed of for years. Years of pain, loneliness, and denial of desire.

You're not afraid of him. You're afraid of falling in love. Lily's words whispered through her mind.

She tried blaming her tension on the fact that the whole resort was on pins and needles now that the wedding was less than twenty-four hours away. But even when she went home in the evenings, the ache went with her. Her body screamed for relief — so long and hard, she'd taken to touching herself at night and imagining it was him.

Whether it was black magic or Hunter's raw masculinity that got her so riled up, she didn't care any more. All she wanted was relief.

"Up there," someone called.

Dawn whipped her head around and cursed at the sight of three figures marching up the hill. Regina Vanderpelt led the charge, wearing movie star sunglasses that covered more skin than her bikini did. Veronica and a hand-wringing resort employee tagged along in her wake.

"I'm sorry, Miss Vanderpelt, but it really isn't possible—"

Regina ignored the man completely. "I want the wedding up here."

"You see that sign?" The man pointed, but the bride looked in the other direction.

"I said, I want my wedding here."

Dawn peeked at the sign that said, *Proceed at your own risk. Do not approach cliff. Rocks may be unstable.*

"The lawn is much better," Veronica tried.

"I don't want a fucking lawn wedding. I came to Hawaii for a beach wedding," Regina snapped.

"I'm afraid that won't be possible," the man said. "That freak storm may be a thousand miles offshore, but the swell is increasing every hour."

Dawn peered at the surf pounding into the rocks below, unperturbed by the vertical drop. If she were an owl, it would be the perfect place to roost. Well — fifty years ago, it would have been. Now that resorts had taken over most of the coast, the native birds had all moved to quieter nesting grounds.

Regina made a face. "I don't care. I want the wedding moved up here. It's the same view. An even better view. And I want it."

"You can fit a lot more guests on the lawn," the man said.

Regina made a face. "I'll just un-invite a few."

Veronica checked her tablet. "You're already down to three hundred. And that's not counting the guests your parents invited."

Regina sniffed. "Crotchety old businessmen. They'd rather spend the day golfing anyway. Besides, I'll look really good in my white dress with the ocean behind me. If that idiot photographer gets the angle right, that is."

Dawn edged downslope, away from Regina's cloud of negative snobbery.

Veronica clucked quietly. "What a tragedy it would be if the rock gave way, taking you and Ricky with it." Her voice had a wistful quality to it.

"You can always bring the groom up here for a photo before the wedding," the man suggested.

Dawn wondered if the groom would sober up enough to manage the uphill climb. Ricky Zappello, the boy-band rock star, had arrived at the resort the day before, more than a little glassy-eyed.

"I don't want a picture. I want the wedding up here," Regina insisted, stamping her foot.

"Whoa—" the man muttered as the ground underfoot shook.

Dawn threw her hands out for balance. Veronica yelped and covered her head as if the sky threatened to fall on her head instead of the cliff giving way under her feet.

"Nobody move," Dawn shouted, praying that, for once, Regina would listen. Because, wow. Either the outcrop really was unstable, or Regina was a lot more powerful than she looked.

Regina's face turned white, but when the shaking stopped, she went back to her usual scowl.

"Hmpf." She turned up her nose and stomped down the hill. "I didn't want my wedding up here anyway."

And off she went on her next battle charge, the amethyst in her engagement ring flashing in the sun. Dawn wondered which unlucky soul would be the butt of Regina's scorn next.

"Come along, Veronica," Regina snipped in the tone she might use with a pet poodle.

Veronica followed, as did the man, who shot Dawn a wide-eyed look.

"I swear she'll give me a heart attack one of these days. The sooner this wedding is over, the better," he muttered.

Somehow, the notion didn't sit well with Dawn. When the wedding was over, her special assignment would be over, too, and then she'd be back to fleeting glances of Hunter on the highway instead of hours spent together on the same job.

She checked her watch as she walked down the hill. Only ten minutes to catch a bite to eat in the tent set up for staff near the wedding site. She snagged one of the last sandwiches off a tray and stepped aside to eat it, wondering if Hunter had taken his break yet.

Employees and security personnel rotated through the tent, murmuring as they flopped down in plastic chairs.

"Another day of this and I'll be so done," someone sighed.

"How much you want to bet that this million-dollar wedding ends in divorce five months down the line?" A man laughed.

"More like five weeks," someone else quipped, and everyone laughed.

"Remind me never to get married like this," a woman said.

"Like you'd have the money to."

"Even if I did, it wouldn't be like this."

"How would you get married?" someone asked, eliciting a flood of ideas — everything from sandbars at low tide to castles in Scotland or even Disneyland.

Right here on Maui, Dawn couldn't help thinking. *A quiet little ceremony, with just a few friends. The ones who really count.*

She closed her eyes, imagining a grassy lawn shaded by palm trees. A pure blue sky. Brown eyes gazing into hers, promising to love her forever.

The flaps at the far side of the tent slapped open, and Hunter and Cruz stalked in. Everyone stopped and stared for a moment. Something about their powerful aura did that every time. Hunter frowned and Cruz scowled, making everyone drop their gazes as if guilty of some crime.

Dawn, though, kept her eyes on Hunter, whose eyes swept over the area and came to rest on hers. Brown eyes just as soft and devoted as the ones in her daydream. His chest rose with a deep, slow breath, and Dawn stared while the conversation around her picked up again.

"I don't think young people know what love is these days," an older woman sighed.

Dawn's pulse skipped. Funny, she had the feeling she did.

"Maybe we should give them the benefit of the doubt."

Dawn bit her lip. Did that apply to a man who could shift into a bear?

"Maybe Regina really meant it about that sex video scandal — that she was just playing around. Maybe she's finally found true love."

An older woman scoffed. "True love is patience. Persistence. Self-sacrifice."

Dawn worked a bite of sandwich down with a dry gulp, studying Hunter.

"True love is when just being close to the person is enough."

Dawn's eyes locked on Hunter's, and time stood still.

"Love is about the little things, not grand gestures," the woman added.

Dawn's hands trembled, and her cheeks warmed. Love should be a vague, undefinable thing, and yet it seemed entirely tangible just then. Love was joy and peace and, yes, a little bit of fear balanced with a great reward.

The older woman sighed, and Dawn did, too.

Then someone snapped their fingers and said, "I need two volunteers. Right now."

"I think those two will be perfect," a man who sounded a lot like Kai said.

"Right. You and you. Come with me."

Someone nudged Dawn, and she ripped her eyes off Hunter. "Who, me?"

Kai stood at the entrance to the party tent, wearing a mischievous grin. The photographer beside him gestured at Dawn and Hunter. "Come on already. This will just take a second."

Hunter balked, as did Dawn, but Kai hustled both of them along. "No need to dally, kids."

Dawn frowned. What was going on? Hunter's nostrils flared like a dog testing the air for an intruder. But there was no disturbance outside the tent, just the section of lawn that had been cordoned off beside the bandstand. What did the photographer want? And why did Kai seem so amused?

The photographer fiddled with a light meter and squinted into the sun. "Over there, please." He motioned Dawn and

Hunter into the center of the square and circled them. Hunter circled too, a wary expression on his face.

"Perfect," the photographer murmured, totally unaware of the bear lurking inside the man he'd just put on high alert. "Now get a little closer. . ."

Dawn's jaw dropped. Hunter looked to Kai, who shrugged.

"Come on. Help a guy out, won't you?" the photographer said in his nasal tone. "I need to check my angles for the wedding party tomorrow. You, put your hand on his shoulder," he said to Dawn. "And you, put your hands on her waist."

Dawn and Hunter stared at each other like a couple of awkward seventh graders at their first dance.

"Don't just stand there. Dance. Honestly, how hard is that?"

If Hunter hadn't looked absolutely petrified, Dawn might have balked. But her heart softened, and she took his hands.

Hunter gulped and looked down, and she did, too. His hands dwarfed hers, but his grip was soft. Perfect, in fact. She stepped a little closer, trying to breathe steadily.

Hunter tipped his chin, following her movements, and his Adam's apple bobbed.

"Better," the photographer murmured, moving around them. His rapid-fire camera clicked away. Then he checked the results and adjusted the setting. "Over there a little more. And I need her on my side."

A low growl built in Hunter's throat, and Dawn might have laughed if she hadn't been holding her breath. Funny that she actually *liked* the feeling of Hunter keeping other men away. She turned slightly for the photographer, squeezing Hunter's hands. The second she did, his eyes softened.

Well, dang. Was that all it took to calm a bear shifter down? A little touch? A smile? She thought back to the day of the shifter battle and filtered through the memories. The image of a murderous bear had pushed every other memory aside, but when she searched deeper, she realized there was more. Hunter had only looked fierce when he'd halted her attacker. Moments later, when he shifted back to human form, all she had seen was sorrow. Deep, deep sorrow through eyes that beseeched her, begging for a chance to explain.

I only want to protect you. To love you. Forever, if you'll let me. Please.

Slowly, she ran her hands up his forearms.

True love is patience. Persistence. Self-sacrifice, the woman in the tent had said.

Dawn took a deep breath, working her hands up to his shoulders. Boy, did he smell nice. Like oak and leather. Like the Kahalawai peaks after a spring shower. Like koa, the toughest kind of wood.

"Just a little more to the right," the photographer murmured.

She stepped right, then put her weight back on her left foot, and then shifted right again, swaying into a pantomime of a dance.

Hunter's arms loosened slightly, and his chest brushed hers. She nestled a little closer.

The speakers squeaked with static, and music started up with an old-fashioned tune that worked its way into her limbs and told them how to move. She'd never been much of a dancer, but wow. It wasn't actually that hard. Not with Hunter there and the music helping her along. It helped him, too, because he gradually loosened up and started swaying to the beat.

"Perfect," the photographer murmured. "Let me just try my other lens..."

Dawn tuned the voice out and concentrated on Hunter instead. The man was rock solid, yet he yielded to the slightest pressure to turn this way or that. His chin was close to her cheek — so, so tempting to nuzzle against.

And oops, she really did sneak in a nuzzle. Or two. Maybe even three, until Hunter tipped his head against hers and snuggled her in even closer, and that was nice, too.

She had the vague feeling that people were watching, but her mind was just blurry enough not to care.

"Okay, just one more shot over here," the photographer said.

Dawn nearly murmured, *No rush.* She could keep this up all day.

Hunter's hands moved over her back, and her imagination ran away with the idea of all the other parts of her body they might wander to. Not that they did, damn it. She pressed her hips against his and felt him nudge back. Her lips parted as she considered kissing his neck, though a fuzzy sensation told her she'd better not — yet. Which was puzzling, because it felt so perfect, squeezing her body against his. Natural. Peaceful, almost. Why should she hold back?

Then a sudden racket sounded behind her, and Hunter lunged around, protecting her body with his.

Dawn's eyes fluttered as she fought to focus. Whew. Where was she? What was happening?

"Sorry," the photographer said sheepishly, stepping away from the chair he'd backed into. "Anyway, that's enough. You can go back to work."

No, she wanted to protest. *I'm not ready yet.*

But then the blood rushed to Dawn's face, and her brain switched back on. Wait — had she just been slow-dancing with Hunter?

His face was as pink as hers must have turned, and they stared at each other, half a step apart. His eyes glowed, and it wasn't a trick of the light.

A lump formed in her throat. She hadn't even realized how close she'd gotten to Hunter. She hadn't felt anything but an inner pull. No fear, no panic gripping her body, telling her to scream and shove him away.

"Hunter," she murmured, not really sure what she wanted to say. *Thank you? Don't let me go? I'm sorry?*

He squeezed her hands, and his lips turned up in a smile.

Chapter Nine

Somehow, Hunter forced himself to step away from Dawn and straighten his tie. Somebody said something, but he didn't catch what, not with his blood roaring through his veins.

Mate, his bear whispered in sheer joy. *She is our mate.*

Well, he already knew that, but Dawn seemed to recognize it, too. She'd snuggled right in and danced with him, and even afterward, when the daze cleared from her eyes, her gaze was steady and warm. Unafraid.

But damn it, people were bustling all around them again, and someone called Dawn away. She went, casting longing looks over her shoulder that made him want to beat his chest and cry, *Mine!*

"Way to go, partner," Kai murmured with a smack to his back.

"Who knew the big lug could dance?" That was Cruz, who didn't sound as grouchy as usual.

Hunter ignored them, keeping his eyes on Dawn. He took a deep breath, savoring the scent of Dawn that still lingered all around. When was the last time he'd felt so good?

It didn't last long, though, because a moment later, a cry broke out, and every muscle in his body tensed again.

"Where is my photographer? Damn it, where is that man?"

"Bridezilla returns," Cruz muttered, beating a hasty retreat.

Kai grabbed Hunter's arm and steered him away from what was sure to be another scene. "The wedding rehearsal will be starting soon. Remember?"

Hunter groaned. How could things go from so good to so miserable in such a short time?

"Listen, I can cover for you until the rehearsal party," Kai started, and Hunter's universe brightened again. "But I promised Tessa I'd be back before eight."

Hunter waited as Kai went on.

"Dawn is going off duty now. Why don't you get a ride home with her? Take a little break."

Hunter checked his watch, then his sanity. Wait. Was he really going to leave his post?

"I said, I can cover for you," Kai said, reading his mind.

Hurry, his bear said, sniffing in the direction Dawn had gone.

So he did hurry. He practically sprinted, in fact, and caught up just as she was getting to her car.

"Dawn," he called, screeching to a stop before he spooked her again. He caught his breath, pretending he wasn't panting.

She whirled, and he feared the worst. But her face brightened when she saw him, and her lips quivered when she said, "Yes?"

Her tone was upbeat. Hopeful, almost.

He clamped his lips together because suddenly, he wasn't sure what to say anymore. Maybe just, *Dawn, can you give me a ride?* Or should he be a little bolder and say what he really felt? *Dawn, I love you desperately. Please, don't let me go.*

He cleared his throat, but all that came out was a jumble.

"I'm off for a few hours. You too?" she asked, coming to his rescue.

He nodded eagerly. Too eagerly?

She leaned on the open car door and considered for a minute. "They want me back for the rehearsal party tonight. In plain clothes," she sighed. "Bride's orders."

For once, Hunter couldn't find fault with one of Regina's wishes. Not that he minded Dawn in uniform — hell, he'd love looking at her if she wore a penguin suit — but the uniform was a constant reminder that she was an officer of the law, and he was a man who occasionally had to operate outside the law, if only when he had good reason to.

"Yeah," he said gruffly. "I'm off for a little while, too."

He held his breath while she considered a second longer. "Would you like a ride home?"

He jerked his head up and down and circled to the passenger seat when she nodded him in. His overeager bear nearly made him dash around the car, but he hit the brakes and walked at what he hoped was a casual pace.

Don't be such a child, he chastised his bear — a little hypocritically, really, because he was equally delighted. He buckled up, leaned back in the seat, and looked around. Holy smokes. He was in a car. With Dawn. Driving. Going someplace — a place he couldn't recall anymore, but it barely seemed to matter.

He sat very still, telling himself not to get too excited. But boy, was that hard. His mind kept flashing back to images of their dance — and worse, overlaying that with memories of their kiss.

"Long day today," she murmured, filling the silence.

"Long day," he agreed.

The window was open, and thank God for that, because he could have passed out just from her heavenly scent. Jasmine and buttercup and hibiscus, all mixed together, along with something new. A scent he couldn't quite place.

Ask her, his bear said. *Go ahead and ask her.*

He sat perfectly still, afraid to say a word. He couldn't ask Dawn what he was dying to say. He didn't dare.

Come on, already, his bear demanded. *Just ask.*

She was just warming up to him again. He'd ruin everything if he pushed too hard.

Wanna bet? his bear said, sniffing deeply.

He closed his eyes, trying to place the new ingredient in her scent, and froze when he realized what it was.

Desire.

He sat very, very still and sniffed again, double-checking. That was definitely the scent of desire. A sweet, cotton-candy scent he often caught wafting between the mated couples of Koa Point — Kai and Tessa, and Boone and Nina.

Dawn and Hunter, his bear murmured, trying their names out side by side. *We even sound like we belong together. And Meli means honey. We're made for each other.*

Ah, the logic of a grizzly. Hunter sighed.

So ask her, already, his inner beast cried.

He'd barely spoken ten words to her today. Make that, over the past days — or weeks, even. There was no way he could express what he felt.

You don't have to be a poet. Just ask, his bear said.

Maybe he should wait until they got to the gate of Koa Point.

His bear rolled its eyes. *Say it. Say, Dawn...*

"Dawn," he said, barely above the sound of the engine.

She turned her head.

Would you like to stop by my place? his bear coached, sounding out the words for his thick brain.

"Would you like to stop by my place?" he whispered.

For a second, he thought she hadn't heard because she just drove along. But then she opened her mouth and shook her head. "No."

His heart sank. *I told you,* he started accusing his bear, but Dawn spoke up, cutting him off.

"No, but I'd like you to stop by my place," she said, quiet as a mouse.

She kept her eyes glued to the road, but he could sense her heart rate accelerate the way he wished the car would.

Say something, idiot, his bear hissed.

"That would be very nice," he managed.

His bear groaned.

What? Hunter demanded.

Is that the best you can do?

He considered. Yes. That was the best he could do. But heck, Dawn didn't seem to mind. In fact, the car's speed inched up as she made a turn inland.

"It's just up here, about two miles," she murmured.

He nodded, pretending his heart wasn't leaping around in glee.

"So, about Lily..." Dawn started.

Right, the landlord. Hunter liked Lily, but he hoped to hell she was out. But if not, okay. He could sit and drink a cup of tea instead of making the most of some private time. As long as he got to stay near Dawn.

"She'll probably be out. It's bridge night," Dawn said.

His heart thumped a little harder, and his pulse spiked. "Bridge night. Nice," he said like a total moron.

Bridge night is great, his bear crooned.

They passed a sugarcane field and a scattering of houses before turning left down a lane of cottages shaded by pines. Dawn parked in front of the blue-shuttered house at the end and sat still for a minute.

"Um, if you don't want to..." he said, though it made his gut churn to imagine her changing her mind now.

She shook her head and stuck on a smile. A brave smile that made him wonder what was going on in her mind. Was it his bear, scaring her again?

She motioned him out of the car and walked briskly down a path along the left side of the house. "That's Lily's place..."

Hunter nodded, thanking every god in the Hawaiian pantheon that the older woman wasn't home.

Dawn pointed to a yellow cottage with white trim around the back. "I rent the place back here..."

"Nice." Somehow, he'd imagined her in exactly such a place. Small, cozy, and neat, with potted plants and a lantern by the door.

The chair on the little porch faced west, where the sun was setting in vivid stripes of red, orange, and yellow. The screen door opened with a squeak, and he held it, trying to hide the shake in his hand while Dawn fumbled with the keys.

"There," she murmured, pushing the door open and gesturing him in.

The place was neat as a pin, of course. Whatever dishes she'd used for breakfast had been dried and put away, and the magazines on the table were arranged just so. Each of the throw pillows on the love seat was offset from the one behind it at exactly the same angle, like a flicked-open fan in various shades of blue.

"Nice," he said, stepping to the floor-to-ceiling bookshelf on one wall. There were books on Hawaiian flowers, Hawaiian quilts, and Hawaiian history arranged by category and set apart by owl figurines of all shapes and sizes. A glittery owl. An owl made out of a coconut. A ceramic owl. Even an owl made out of seashells.

Hoo, hoo. Right on cue, an owl hooted from outside.

Pu'eo is Dawn's aumakua, he remembered Lily saying. The form her ancestral spirit took.

"Wow," he said, spotting a basalt poi pounder by the loveseat.

"I'm kind of a flea market junkie," Dawn said, pointing to the antique Victrola in the corner.

"Does that work?"

"Sure does," she said, lifting the lid and cranking the handle. She carefully placed the needle on the record and let it spin. "The song takes a second to start up," Dawn murmured as the scratchy sound of an old-time 78 record filled the room with quiet anticipation.

The door to the bedroom was ajar — the only other room under the peaked roof — and Hunter couldn't help glancing in. His breath caught when he saw the quilt on the four-poster bed. A bright, yellow quilt with a flowery pattern.

"Oh."

"What?" She came up to his shoulder and looked, too.

"My mom had a quilt a lot like that."

A slew of sounds, sights, and smells washed over him. The babble of the creek beside the cabin he'd grown up in. The fresh scent of wildflowers in spring. The sunny yellow of his mother's old dress, recycled as patches in the quilt.

He turned away from the memories so quickly that he nearly bumped into Dawn, and he caught her arms — more to steady himself than her. They stared at each other for a second, and then, without thinking, he pulled her into a hug. A hug that had nothing to do with *steady* anything, because his heart was pounding away.

He started to pull back, afraid of how Dawn would react, but her arms slid around him and tightened, refusing to let go.

"This is good." Her voice was muffled, and his chest heated under the spot closest to her face.

"It is good," he whispered, resting his head on hers.

They stood there for a long minute while the Victrola needle went around and around, and he wasn't entirely sure what to do. Not sure he *wanted* to do anything, because just holding her was great. But when her hands started moving along his back, his bear gave him all kinds of bad ideas.

She wants this, too. No need to hold back.

Of course, he had to hold back. No way was he going to risk scaring her again. Not that she seemed all that scared, which figured. Dawn was as tough as they came, even if she reminded him of an exotic flower.

The song on the phonograph kicked in with a slow, soft island tune from the thirties. One of those happy, ukulele tunes with just enough of a beat to it that their bodies started to sway.

"On a little bamboo bridge," Dawn whispered.

He took a deep breath, relishing the press of her chest against his. Her hands rubbed up and down his back, waking every nerve, and it was all he could do not to grind his hips against hers.

They circled slowly, taking tiny steps in time with the tune.

"Hunter," she whispered, slowly raising her face to his.

Her eyes were bottomless pools of black that shone like pearls, and her lips moved.

Kiss her, his bear prompted.

Slowly, giving her every chance to protest, he lowered his chin. But she didn't pull away. She drew nearer. A moment later, their lips met, and little zips of lightning raced through his veins.

Heaven. Just like that, Hunter was transported to heaven. Dawn's lips danced over his. Every move she made, he mirrored, from the slide of her hand along his ribs to the upward pull of her lips. Her mouth cracked open, and his did, too, letting her taste him. She broke away long enough to grab a deep breath, then dove back in, sweeping her tongue over his teeth.

Her hips swiveled against his, and the scent of arousal spiked, rising above the scent of gardenia wafting in from outside.

He nearly groaned. In fact, he did groan, and his knees buckled slightly, making his groin bump her hip. That set off a whole different brushfire in his body, and he had no choice but to tip his head up toward the ceiling and count to ten.

"No good?" she whispered.

He shook his head immediately. "Really good. Just trying not to rush this."

She laughed, making his bear cheer. "Well, we do only have..." She checked her watch. "Two and a half hours." Her voice was light and playful, but a second later, it grew grave. "Listen. I really want this, Hunter. I want you. But I don't know... I mean, I'm not sure how far... I mean..."

He caught her hands and pressed them to his chest, anchoring her there. "We stop the second you want to. We go as far as you want, but no further."

Her cheeks flushed. The music hit a flirty high note, then went back to its gentle swing.

Dawn swung, too, her hips moving with unmistakable need against his. But while her body seemed all in, she was still hesitant. It showed in her dilated eyes, in the way her mouth opened and closed.

"I've never actually... I mean, I feel ready, but part of me..." She kept starting and stopping, not making any sense.

He held her gently by the shoulders and searched her eyes.

She pulled in a deep breath. "I've never been with a man before." For a second, she stood there, apprehensive of his reaction. "I mean, I've never slept with anyone."

He couldn't help but gape at her. Dawn was a virgin? No way. A woman that confident, that beautiful must have had sex with someone somewhere along the line — or so he'd assumed.

Then it hit him. That bastard football player back in high school. Had he left Dawn with scars that deep?

I told you we should have killed him on the spot, his bear grumbled.

He closed his eyes, remembering it all. The unsettled, itchy sensation that had him backtrack to the shed at the end of the school fields. The nauseating scene he discovered when he flung the door open and found that ass of a quarterback, Clive, lying over Dawn, tearing at her clothes. Her small fists had been pummeling Clive's back with no effect, and she'd worn a look of sheer terror. When Hunter flung Clive across the shed and pulled Dawn to her feet, she shook all over and tears streaked down her face.

Hunter always figured fate had guided him to Dawn just in the nick of time, but maybe he'd been a little too late. That rat bastard, Clive, had done damage of a different kind. Clive had stolen one of life's purest pleasures from Dawn, and that wasn't right.

God, she was tough, never letting on as to how deeply she'd been scarred. And shit, what an asshole he was for assuming she'd simply put the brutal memories behind her.

"We can stop. We can—"

Dawn shook her head vehemently. "I want this, Hunter. I really do. But I think I might have to rush this part. To get over the hump. You know..."

No, he didn't know, but hell. He'd do anything she wanted, even if that meant stopping cold.

"I need to... I need..." She searched for words then muttered, "Aw, hell," and dove back into a kiss. A kiss so out of the blue, she ended up pressing him against the wall. Her hands were everywhere — on his chest, his waist, his back — and all he could do was prop his hands on her shoulders and let her go.

Her kiss grew harder, hungrier. She pulled his shirttail out of his pants to touch his skin. He held his breath as her soft hands traveled over his chest, caressing him the way he longed to caress her. But he couldn't. Dawn needed to take the lead, and he had to follow.

Even if it kills me, his bear agreed, clenching its teeth.

Her hands loosened his tie and fluttered over the buttons of his shirt. She couldn't quite work them open, so he took over while her hands slid down a long, sensual trail and tucked into the back pockets of his pants.

"Good idea," she murmured between kisses as he worked the buttons down. She smoothed her hands over his shoulders, pushing the shirt back.

They were definitely out of time with the scratchy tune on the Victrola, but Hunter couldn't have cared less. When Dawn got to work on her own shirt, all he could do was watch as she revealed more and more of the creamy skin at her neckline, then the edge of her bra. It was white and a little frilly at the edge, a hidden hint of feminine that contrasted with her uniform.

"What are you looking at, mister?" she teased with false bravado, working the rest of the buttons down.

Looking at the woman I love, he nearly said. *An amazing woman who hides her fears — and her desires.*

"Looking at the real you," he murmured.

"You think you know the real me?"

For years, he'd assumed he had. Now, he wasn't so sure. But damn, would he love to devote years to understanding what made her tick.

He tilted his hand from side to side. "I'd like to find out."

Her lips tightened. "What if you don't like what you find?" Her eyes dimmed as if she had a dark secret. But hell — he had plenty of his own. Secrets and scars he'd like to drag out and erase with her help, one by one.

But not tonight. Tonight was about taking the next step.

Sex! his bear cheered.

No, sex wasn't the next step. Not in and of itself. Building trust was, and he needed that as badly as Dawn did.

No sex? his bear cried, confused.

Yes, sex. Well, hopefully. Just don't get it mixed up with what really counts.

Sure. Fine. Whatever, his bear muttered. He sniffed deeply, getting high on her scent.

"You mean you're not perfect?" he said, answering her question at last.

Dawn scoffed. "Far from."

"Good," he murmured, pushing the shirt over her shoulders. "Then I won't feel completely outclassed."

She looked shocked, as if she'd never really stopped to consider what a class act she was, and he chuckled, tossing the garment aside. Then he caught her hands and guided them back to his chest, dying for her to touch him again.

I'm dying to touch her, his bear groaned, because there she was, the woman of dreams, wearing nothing but a nicely filled bra, right in front of his eyes. Her chest heaved, teasing him.

Go slow, he told his bear.

He looped his hands behind her neck and gently worked her hair out of its braid. The long, black strands were just as silky as they were in his dreams, and he finger-combed them again and again.

Nice, his bear mumbled. *Nice.*

Her eyebrow arched in a question, and he nodded. Yes, he'd been dreaming of doing that for years.

His bear fast-forwarded to a scene several years down the line in which Dawn came home from work, flopped wearily on the love seat, and let him finger-comb her hair. *How was your day?* he'd ask, massaging her shoulders. And he'd be the happiest man on earth because he got to be the one to hear her out, each and every day.

He cleared his throat and put the brakes on before he got ahead of himself — way ahead of himself. With one shaky finger, he guided back the strands that had fallen in front of her face. Then he leaned in and kissed her.

Dawn met him eagerly, whimpering into the kiss and inching her hands toward his slacks. She hesitated at the waistline then reached lower, palming his cock through the fabric.

Hunter tipped his head back and surged forward on the balls of his feet, letting the pressure build. He flattened his hands on the wall on either side of her head — careful not to cage Dawn in, but to steady himself. To hang on to that little bit of self-control.

She splayed her fingers and stroked, making him groan. Then slowly, gingerly, she lowered his fly and snaked her hand in. Her eyes went wide, and there it was again — that sense of hesitation, that dichotomy of holding back when she really wanted to dive in. Finally, she gripped him fully and mumbled something unintelligible into the kiss.

Hunter jerked forward and back, rocking on his heels. He could have closed his eyes and continued until he came in her hand, but he forced himself to stop. This wasn't about physical pleasure. This was about bonding with his mate.

He opened his eyes slowly, afraid that the aroused glow might frighten Dawn. But she met his eyes easily and tipped up her chin.

"Touch me," she whispered, pulling his hands toward her breasts.

Hunter bit his lip, telling himself to go slow, but Dawn's eyes flashed.

"Don't," she said, making him stop cold.

He steeled every muscle and stopped instantly. Shit, this was it. She'd changed her mind.

Dawn shook her head and shaped his hands into cups under her breasts. "I mean, don't stop. Please. Don't stop."

Chapter Ten

For a woman with a compulsive need to maintain control, Dawn decided she was doing a pretty good job of letting go. Or maybe it was Hunter making her feel so secure, she forgot to be afraid. She forgot to care that the record had reached its end, leaving the needle to travel in endless circles, around and around. She forgot about everything but the burning need in her soul.

What you need is someone to shake you out of that carefully controlled cage you live in.

Someone like Hunter.

Without love, you don't live. Lily's words had never seemed truer than now.

She could sense the power and raw need in Hunter, and yet his huge hands were gentle — so gentle, she wanted to yowl and beg for more. Hunter was nothing like the pawing, panting man she'd once fought off. And when he touched the hypersensitive skin of her breasts, she groaned.

"So good..."

He pressed closer and started kissing her ear while massaging her breasts — circular motions around the sides mixed with little flicks of his thumbs over the front. She writhed under his touch, squeezing closer to him.

"Please, Hunter. Take it off," she murmured as his hands played over her bra.

He did so with the look of a museumgoer studying a new masterpiece. In the end, she was the one who yanked the fabric off her shoulders and tossed it to the side. Hunter's breath caught, but he touched her again, and the next swipe of his coarse thumbs was exactly the ecstasy she thought it would be.

"So good," she murmured, again and again.

For years, she'd avoided intimacy. How could she trust any man after her near-rape? And worse, how could she satisfy the man she loved if she couldn't stand the thought of being touched?

It was a curse. Her body craved sex as much as any other woman's, but it repelled the urge at the same time.

Until now. Now, she was hungry. Starving. And absolutely, totally sure that with Hunter, sex would be an act of beauty instead of a crime.

When she ran her hands along his hard abs and wrapped a leg around his side, he groaned and went still. His cock jutted against her belly through the fabric of his boxers, and his breath came a little faster.

"You're sure, right?" he croaked.

Holy hell, was she sure. This was so much more than she'd ever dreamed it would be. She had always figured sex meant a woman giving up control to a man, but Hunter ceded all power to her. That incredible, animal power pulsing under his skin wasn't an offensive weapon she ought to fear. It was pure defense, only brought into action to protect her.

She gulped. Hunter had gone to war to protect his country. And now all he wanted, it seemed, was to protect her. Even completely aroused, he was holding back, unwilling to push her too far.

She pushed his pants farther down and fisted his cock. The more Hunter held back, the more confidence she gained. She could do this. She could enjoy a man's touch. Well, at least *this* man's touch. It set her free.

He closed his eyes and groaned her name. Half a step to the right was the entrance to her bedroom, and she considered the threshold quietly. Stepping over it with Hunter represented much more than just a physical step. Was she really ready for that?

Yes, her body cried. *Yes, please.*

"Hunter," she whispered, helping him shuck the pants then pulling him through the bedroom door. When they crossed the invisible line, she exhaled. No panic, no nightmarish images from the past. Just Hunter, caressing her skin.

She stepped backward until her calves bumped the bed, where she slowly lay back. Hunter followed, his wide shoulders blocking her view of most of the room. He came down on all fours over her, and for one awful, out-of-the-blue moment, her body locked up, bringing her back to the past. But when Hunter murmured her name and nuzzled her chin gently, the panic disappeared. His beard was ridiculously soft, tickling her skin. When she giggled in relief, he popped up to look at her.

"What?"

She tugged him back into place and nuzzled back. "I like that."

"Good," he rumbled, kissing and nuzzling his way to her left ear then the right. Then he started working his way down her body, one inch at a time.

Dawn went from sighs of pleasure to cries of delight, and she arched her back. Was that shifter magic at work or was it just his close-cropped beard and incredibly soft lips, driving her wild?

His chin continued on its sensual path, scraping over her belly then along her right thigh.

"This okay?" he murmured, letting his hands whisper over her skin.

Her knees flopped open, answering before she could get out a word. She clutched the sheets and nodded, keeping her eyes shut tight.

Please, don't let me ruin this now. Please, no nightmares, she begged.

If her libido had its own voice, it would have scoffed. *This is Hunter. He's incapable of making me feel anything but good.*

He did make her feel good, especially when his hands swept slowly between her legs. The more he nuzzled her thighs and hip, the more heat pooled between her legs. She was so slick, his fingers slid right through her folds, and her knees split wider.

"Oh... Yes..." she moaned, aching for more.

He probed deeper, and Dawn closed her eyes, remembering all the lonely, heated nights when she'd resorted to touching herself. It had always helped, but wow — having Hunter touch

ANNA LOWE

her was exponentially better. His fingers dipped in and out of her, making her pant and writhe.

When she tilted her head back, Hunter moved back up her body, working her breasts with his lips while his hand stayed tucked between her legs, moving faster all the time. His cock was hard and high against her hip, and a drop of moisture formed.

"So good..." she moaned. "Hunter, please." She wrapped her leg around his, trying to get him aligned. She was ready. So, so ready.

He hesitated long enough to make her open her eyes.

"What?"

"I don't have a condom," he rasped.

She laughed out loud and rolled to the bedside table while he looked on in surprise.

"Yes, I have condoms. Wishful thinking, believe me," she explained, handing him the unopened package. A few months earlier, when her dreams involving Hunter had gone from sweet to sultry, she'd purchased the condoms, hoping that would help break down her mental barriers until someday...

She gulped, watching Hunter open the package. Someday had finally arrived.

As he unrolled it over himself, her eyes went wide. When she dipped a hand down to help, he seemed to double in girth. Was he really going to fit inside her?

Hunter touched her again, coating himself with her moisture.

"Slow," she whispered.

No — fast! the cat-in-heat part of her body screamed. *Fast and hard.*

Hunter came down over her, his knees between hers. With his left hand, he guided his cock through her folds. She thought he was doing that for his own pleasure, but the way he groaned under his breath made her realize he was holding back. Controlling himself.

The moment she realized it, a switch flipped inside her. Control sucked. Control was a crutch for the timid, and she was not afraid. Not anymore. Not of Hunter.

The next time his cock dragged over her entrance, she bucked up, enveloping him.

Hunter jerked to a stop, but she grabbed his shoulders and pulled with her legs. "Now, Hunter. I need you so much."

One huge bicep flexed beside her as he slowly lowered himself, plunging deeper. The inner push hurt, but it felt good, too, and she moved her lips in silent cries.

"More," she begged.

Hunter pulled back a tiny bit before nudging deeper again. His head came down beside hers, and his shoulders shook from sheer strain.

"Is this okay?" he asked in a choked voice.

A shot of pure appreciation filled her body, erasing any pain. What further proof did she need of this man's willingness to put her above himself?

"I'm good. God, am I good," she managed.

He pushed deeper still, filling her with heat. Moving faster as she grew slicker inside. At one point, she winced at a tear of sudden pain, but after that, it was pure pleasure. Hunter pulled back then pushed back in, making her toss her head back and moan. When he started pumping in and out of her, her body moved instinctively, matching his rhythm. Her garbled cries filled the room, but she didn't care one bit.

Ecstasy. So this is what that word means, she thought as her whole body exalted in the burning sensation.

Hunter combed her hair back from her face so they could lock eyes. His glowed the way overheated bricks might — a deep, reddish brown — and sweat formed at his brow. He thrust faster, leaning left and right, stretching her exquisitely and driving hard along her inner walls. Then his eyes grew darker, and his teeth clenched.

"Soon," he murmured, squeezing her hands. Not pinning her in place so much as anchoring her.

Soon was good, because her body was soaring along on a high that threatened to spiral out of control. Her muscles clamped down one by one to squeeze his cock, making him groan.

"Is that okay?"

He nodded feverishly. "Do it again. Please, do it again."

Clearly, she was the rookie, but the need in his voice made her glow. She was doing it right. She was making him feel good, too.

When she took a deep breath and clenched, Hunter shuddered inside. His movement grew jerkier, his brow shiny with sweat.

"Yes," she started chanting as he pumped into her hard enough to make the four-poster bed squeak. "Yes..."

She closed her eyes, tuning in completely to sensation. That much power, sliding inside her. That much desire, focused on her. That strong a connection. She rolled her head from side to side, locking down over him one more time.

"Hunter," she cried.

His next thrust was his deepest, and they both howled. Her vision dimmed as a wave of pleasure rolled through her body, making her shudder and cry. Thick layers of muscle stiffened throughout his body as he came at the very same moment she did.

"So good," she whispered, wanting to wallow in this wild pleasure as long as she could. Her muscles unwound, one by one, and she melted into the mattress.

"Hunter," she murmured, running her hands over his back.

He held her through an aftershock of pleasure, whispering her name. She convulsed, exulting in the feeling each time. When she stopped shaking, she melted into Hunter's arms, fighting back tears. Why had she been afraid for so long? Why had she shielded herself in a false feeling of control when letting go was so much better?

"Hey," he whispered, running a finger along her jaw. "You okay?"

She rested her cheek against his chest and sighed the deepest sigh of her life. "More than okay." She laced her fingers through his, unwilling to separate from him.

He nuzzled her then rolled, making her protest.

"Sorry. I need to get rid of this," he murmured, heading for the bathroom with the condom.

The bed felt emptier and colder without Hunter. The needle of the Victrola scratched around and around in the sudden silence. But even that produced a tune, in a way. She glanced at the condom package. How many more did she have? And how long would they have to wait before going for another round? She checked the clock. God, where had the time gone?

Hunter detoured to lift the needle from the record before sliding under the sheets and spooning her from behind. He kissed her shoulder then nuzzled it with his cheek, reminding her he was more than a man. He was a bear shifter.

She waited for apprehension to set in, but all she felt was spine-tingling satisfaction. The bear part was... Well, maybe *cute* would be going too far. But sexy, for sure. Having a man who harbored an inner beast had its own special appeal. He was like a life-sized teddy bear — but nothing like a teddy bear, because his body did the most amazing things to hers. Just listening to his voice rumble made her toes curl.

"Thank you," he said, so quietly, she had to strain to make out the words.

She turned in his arms and cupped his face. "No, thank you."

The kiss she planted on his lips was sweet, slow, and absolutely perfect. When she gradually drew back and made it into a nose snuggle, that felt good, too. So good, she wondered why people didn't go on about the afterglow as much as they did about actual sex.

She ended up gazing into his eyes with what had to be a goofy smile while he shook his head.

"What?" she asked.

His lips turned up in one of those rare little-boy smiles she loved so much. "Pinch me," he laughed, brushing the back of his knuckles along her arm.

Dawn bit her lip. Yes, it was a *pinch me, I'm dreaming* moment for her, too.

"You have no idea how long I wanted this," she confessed quietly, hiding her face against his chest.

"Wanna bet?" His chest rose and fell with a sigh.

She laughed, popping her head up. "I can't believe we have Regina Vanderpelt to thank for something."

He chuckled then turned his eyes to the left. An owl hooted outside, sounding perfectly content. A lot like her. She didn't even feel the slightest urge to tidy up the clothes and sheets strewn around the room.

"You have an owl nesting around here?"

She grinned. "Yep. My *aumakua* likes to keep an eye on me."

People from outside the islands never really understood about ancestral spirits, but Hunter seemed to. He reached over and rearranged the sheets around her, creating a little nest for the two of them. Perfect timing, because her body was cooling off, and she could feel the night's chill. The house was just high enough upslope to feel a temperature difference from the coast. Hunter's fingers alternated between playing over her skin and over the tiny stitches of the quilt.

"Did you make this?"

She shook her head. "My grandmother did. I'm nowhere near as good as her." She pointed to her latest work in progress across the room — a white-and-yellow plumeria appliqué that had taken months just to reach the halfway mark.

"Beautiful," he murmured, though she had the sneaking suspicion his eyes were on her, not the quilt. His arms tightened as he went on. "I remember my mom humming while she quilted. She used to tuck me in under one and sing."

Dawn stroked the thick arms curled around her body. She'd never heard Hunter mention his mother before. Both his parents had died sometime before he came to Maui to live with Georgia Mae, but that was all she knew.

"Do you still have that quilt?" she asked. Quietly. Carefully. Hoping he had good memories mixed in with the bad.

Apparently, not too many, because his body tightened all over again. "No. Jericho Deroux burned our place down along with everything in it."

A vein in his arm pulsed, and she gulped. Had his mother died in the fire, too?

She hugged him tightly and rocked a tiny bit. Suddenly, so much about Hunter made sense. That subtle sadness he always carried with him. The hollow eyes of a boy who missed home. The rigid politeness that came from holding fiercely to lessons he'd been taught a long time ago. His gentleness and penchant for taking care of others, like the kitten he'd taken home. Like her.

She shook her head. Whoever Jericho Deroux was, she hoped he was rotting in jail. Then she reeled herself back from negative thoughts, as she did on the toughest days of her job.

"So much pain in the world, but so much beauty, too."

He forced a thin smile and touched her cheek. "Yeah. That much is true."

Her breasts were mashed against his chest, her hands wandering without her even realizing it. But the moment she became aware of it — whew. That hot, thumping feeling rushed back into her veins. Hunter's eyes sparkled, and a moment later, they were kissing again. And not just kissing but touching and licking until they were all worked up again.

Dawn glanced at the clock then at Hunter, who'd paused in the light nibbles he'd been planting on her breast.

She laughed and went back to kissing his ear. "We still have over an hour, and you know what?"

"What?" he murmured, looking up.

She arched her back, making her nipple rise to within reach of his lips. "I intend to use it well."

Chapter Eleven

Hunter waited on the porch while Dawn dressed, rubbing his shoulder absently against the doorframe. He stopped the moment he realized what he was doing, because this wasn't his turf to mark. It was Dawn's, and while she'd opened up to him, she hadn't exactly begged him to make her his.

What if we beg her to make us hers? his bear tried. *Would that work?*

He grinned, because — yeah, he was that over the moon in love. The best feeling in the world, even if it did come with a sense of gnawing dread. He had far too many hopes and fears on the line, and there was so much he and Dawn had to discuss. Neither of them had brought up the subject of his shifter side, and he hadn't dared to introduce the notion of destined mates.

Surely, she feels it, just like we do. Surely, she knows.

Hunter took a deep breath. Right now, he ought to be relishing the present, not worrying about the future.

He sniffed deeply, inhaling the rich scent of Maui by night. The scent of sex was still in the air, too — faint, but perfectly clear to his keen bear nose — and his chest puffed out a little bit.

Footsteps tapped over the wooden floorboards of the cottage, and he turned.

"Do I look okay?" Dawn asked, stepping onto the porch.

His jaw dropped, and he stood dumbstruck for a long minute. When he finally got his mouth into gear, all that came out were unintelligible sounds. Because, wow. She looked like a million bucks. Well, Dawn always looked like a million bucks, even in her police uniform. But now. . .

An ivory qipao dress sheathed her gentle curves — a gorgeous, body-hugging silk masterpiece that brought out her Asian heritage. Three knot buttons swept from her neck to one shoulder, and a long slit ran up the left leg. Hunter had never cracked open a fashion magazine, but hell, he could picture her fitting right in. No, wait — she'd be on the cover, for sure. Her glossy black hair was plaited in one long braid that fell forward over her left shoulder. The low pumps she wore matched the pure red of her lips, and a pair of dangly earrings sparkled in the moonlight.

"It's... You're... I mean..." He stammered away while his inner bear rolled its eyes.

Say, it's beautiful. You're beautiful. Come on already!

"You look great," he managed at last.

She looked down at herself and twisted her lips uncertainly. "I'm supposed to fit in tonight, but I'm not sure I can match what Regina's guests are likely to be wearing."

He shook his head vehemently. "You'll outshine every one of them. Even without the dress. I mean..."

Dawn laughed and stepped closer. "I think I'd better keep the dress on. At least while we're at work."

His heart soared, and he hoped he wasn't reading too much into her words. They did imply a *later*, right? The time after work when the two of them could...

He cleared his throat hastily and plucked a single flower from the hibiscus growing beside the porch. "Maybe just one more accessory," he murmured, tucking it behind her ear.

He pulled back to look her over then nodded. "Perfect."

Understatement of the year, but Dawn didn't seem to mind. She grinned, meeting his eyes. Then her expression grew soft and serious, and she leaned forward for a kiss.

Lucky for him, kissing Dawn came instinctively, unlike talking. Their lips met and moved slowly together in perfect harmony, and his whole body warmed. He closed his eyes because feeling *and* seeing so much beauty would have completely short-circuited his mind.

Dawn opened her mouth, deepening the kiss, and his arms tugged her tighter.

"Oops," she murmured, pulling gently away. "You'll smudge my lipstick."

Hunter took a deep breath and tried to remind himself about things like work, duty, and appearing respectable. But damn, was that hard, especially when his bear could only think of one thing.

Back to bed. Need to please my mate. Make her mine.

A three-point plan his body was totally on board with, if only they had time. But there was a hell of a lot more at stake tonight than smudged lipstick. Regina Vanderpelt's ring ought to be delivered at any time, what with the wedding the next day. And if the diamond turned out to be one of the Spirit Stones, who knew what hell might break loose in the shifter world?

He took Dawn's hand, trying not to squeeze too tightly as they walked to the car. A dozen ugly scenarios raced through his mind, most of them ending the way the last Spirit Stone caper had — with him forced to shift to bear form in the thick of a fight and Dawn repulsed by the creature he had become.

His bear let out a low, sad whine. *Please don't make me hide again. Please don't lock me away.*

"What did you say?" Dawn turned.

He sealed his lips, muffling the sound. "Nothing."

He glossed over the fib by walking around the car to open the driver's side door for her and leaning down for one more kiss once she was in. Then he circled back to the passenger side and folded his big frame into the compact Japanese car. Dawn drove in silence down the lane and onto the road that led down toward the coast, where she slowed and took his hand.

"Beautiful night," she murmured, nodding over the sea.

Moonlight glittered in a long, wavering line across the Pacific. The sea was heaving from the monster swell that had been building all day, but from this distance, it appeared serene. The pines on the side of the road swayed gently to and fro, and stars sparkled overhead.

Hunter raised Dawn's hand to his lips and kissed her knuckles. "Really beautiful. Almost perfect."

101

ANNA LOWE

When she sighed and drove on, Hunter watched the
sparkling sea and tried to get his head around what lay ahead.
If he was lucky, the wedding ring was just an expensive rock
for the spoiled daughter of an oil tycoon, not a Spirit Stone.
If that was the case, the whole circus at the Kapa'akea resort would wrap up in another forty-eight hours, and he could
concentrate on wooing his mate.

But a good soldier didn't count on luck — and neither did
a bear shifter, not when his mate was involved.

"What do you know about the diamond?" he asked.

Dawn's eyebrow arched. "What do you know about it?"

He bit his lip. Shoot. Whatever she knew about the diamond, police protocol probably forbade her from disclosing.
And whatever she did know about it was unlikely to include
the notion of a Spirit Stone.

He flexed his hands, and the knuckles cracked. Shifters
didn't have a written code, but they had their own protocol
when it came to sensitive information like the power of the
Spirit Stones. So he couldn't divulge anything either. But,
damn. If the diamond was a Spirit Stone, he had to warn
Dawn.

The silence between them stretched on — too long, threat-
ening to damage trust so long in the making. Dawn had trusted
him with so much already. Couldn't he trust her?

Silas's face flashed into his mind, red with fury as he bellowed, *You told her what?*

Hunter squirmed in his seat. He loved his shifter brothers,
but he loved Dawn, too.

A moment later, his decision was made. He'd hidden
enough from Dawn in the past. It was time to come clean.

"Remember the fight?" he whispered, figuring he didn't
have to specify which one. The scene must have been burned
into her mind — all those dead bodies, and him standing there
in bear form.

Dawn's hand stiffened and pulled away from his. She nodded grimly.

"Kramer and his mercenaries were trying to kidnap Nina.
In part for her money, and in part for the ruby she inherited."

102

Dawn's lips barely moved when she spoke. "That six-million-dollar ruby?"

Hunter itched to hold her hand again, but he didn't dare invade her space. "The ruby is worth a lot more than that."

Dawn looked at him sharply. "More than six million?"

He shook his head. "Not what you can count in money. The ruby is a Spirit Stone. It has..." He scratched his head, trying to figure out a way to explain. "It has special powers."

"What kind of powers?"

He ran his teeth over his lower lip. "Powers most humans aren't aware of. But for shifters..."

Dawn's shoulders tensed, but he had to go on.

"There are five Spirit Stones. The ruby is one of them. There's an emerald, too. You remember that helicopter crash on Molokini?"

She gave a terse nod.

"That wasn't just a crash. It was a dragon fight — a fight over Tessa and the emerald."

She hit the brakes. "What do you mean, a dragon fight over Tessa?"

"Well, another dragon wanted her as his mate, and—"

She stared at him. "A *dragon* wanted her as his *what*?"

"Shifters believe in destined mates — finding the one person who's meant for you. The one your heart is bound to forever, who you'll love to the end of your days."

Dawn turned white. "Does the woman get a choice in this?"

His stomach turned. The evening had been so perfect, and now he was messing it all up. "Of course, she does. She recognizes her mate. Tessa loves Kai. She felt the pull as much as he did. But this other dragon came along and..."

"And?" Her hand tightened over the gear stick.

He motioned vaguely in the air. "The other dragon challenged Kai. He wanted Tessa for himself. But the point is—"

Her mutter cut him off. "It sounds like medieval times."

Hunter had to admit she had a point there. Some aspects of the shifter world were on the barbarian end of things. But other parts — like the pure, undying love of a shifter for his destined mate — that eclipsed any of the wonders of the human world.

So tell her. Explain, his bear urged.

Hunter clenched the armrest so tight, his knuckles turned white. Dawn was already on the defensive, and she might not appreciate the difference between a crazed, stalker type and an honest bear who'd sacrifice anything for his mate.

She started driving again, faster than before, as if in a rush to get to the resort where she could give him the boot.

"Dawn, the Stones have great power," he said, trying to guide the conversation back to where it had started. "They call to each other."

Dawn looked up, startled, but didn't utter a word.

"It's possible that Regina's diamond is a Spirit Stone. And if it is, there could be other shifters after it."

"After it?" she demanded. "Is that what you and Cruz are doing? Casing the joint in case the diamond turns out to be more than just a diamond?"

"No!" Hunter sputtered. "We're not after anything. We were hired as security, and that's what we'll do."

"But if the diamond is one of these special stones? Then what?"

"We make sure the enemy doesn't get it."

"And who exactly is the enemy?"

He wrinkled his nose. The shifter world was filled with alliances and feuds, some of which dated back centuries. And like humans, there were good shifters, evil shifters — like the powerful dragon lord, Drax, and everything in between. There were other supernatural species, too. Vampires. Witches.

Hybrids, his bear added in a low growl.

Hybrids. Humans with enough shifter blood to boast the same powers — the incredible strength, the longevity, the ability to heal from most mortal wounds. Everything except the ability to shift. Jericho Deroux, the man who'd killed his parents, was a hybrid. A ruthless man who eliminated innocent families like weeds if they stood in the way of his plans.

"The enemy is anyone who would use the Spirit Stone to heighten his own powers," he said at last.

"What would you do?"

He scratched his head. He'd never really thought it through that far. "I wouldn't do anything with it. I'd just hide it so no one could abuse its powers."

"Hide it? Where?"

He made a face. Silas was a dragon, and dragons kept treasure hoards. He would have a safe place to store the diamond, for sure. But Silas would kill Hunter if he revealed such a secret to Dawn, so again, he was stuck.

He settled for a vague flap of the hand. "The point is to keep it away from evil."

"But the diamond is Regina's." Dawn pointed out. "And though I'm no fan, I wouldn't exactly call her evil."

"It is Regina's. And hopefully, it's not a Spirit Stone, and there's no issue."

"But if it is a Spirit Stone?"

Hunter considered. "If it is and no other shifter catches on, we do nothing. Silas says the Spirit Stones slumber."

"Slumber?"

Yeah, it sounded funny to him, too. Such an innocent word for such a powerful object. "As long as they slumber, they're basically off the radar. It's only those brief periods when they change hands that their powers awake and cause trouble."

"Trouble. Right." She frowned.

"If nothing disturbs the Spirit Stone, it will go on slumbering, and no shifter will take notice of it. Regina can have it, no problem — well, other than regular human thieves, I guess. But someday, when it changes hands, the danger arises again. The stone could awaken and attract trouble."

Dawn put a hand to her cheek and scratched hard. If she hadn't been driving, he could imagine her rubbing both eyes in disbelief.

He dragged a hand through his hair. Why had he even brought the subject up?

Because Dawn needs to know for her own safety, his bear said.

He took a deep breath. "Look, just keep the possibility in mind, and stay safe, all right?"

"I'm a police officer, Hunter." Defiance tinged her voice. "I might be undercover, but when I'm on the job, I do my job. You get that?"

He looked at her. Shit. That sense of connection was gone, and Dawn was back to being cool, professional Officer Meli. Had he just wrecked everything by bringing up the diamond?

"I get it," he whispered. "I get it."

They drove in a silence so fraught with tension, Hunter didn't dare move a muscle. When they reached the resort, Dawn parked in a hurry and slammed her door.

"I have to check on something," she murmured, hurrying away.

He let out a breath — the one he felt like he'd been holding throughout the latter part of the drive — and let his shoulders slump.

"So, how did it go?" Kai asked, appearing out of nowhere to smack Hunter on the back.

Hunter kicked the dirt. The evening had been a dream come true until he'd fucked everything up.

"Your timing is perfect," Kai said with a yawn. "I need to head back— Whoa." He sniffed deeply.

Hunter's spine went ramrod straight. Dragons might not have noses as keen as bears, but they could pick up the fresh scent of sex. Hunter had showered, but the scent still clung to him.

Kai cracked into a huge grin. "Way to go. You and Dawn finally—"

Hunter whirled and shoved Kai back, glowering.

"But that's good, right?" Kai asked, confused. "I mean..." He trailed off.

Hunter straightened his tie and checked his watch. "How did the rehearsal go?"

Kai looked at him wordlessly before finally giving in to the change of topic. "I guess you can say it went in true Regina style. A couple of hissy fits, lots of photos. The usual. The groom looks like he's having second thoughts, and who can blame him? But, yeah. They made it through the rehearsal. I'm not sure they'll make it through the wedding, though."

"What about the ring?" Hunter asked, dropping his voice.

Kai shook his head. "It arrived with what looks to be the security team of Fort Knox. I managed to get a look at the diamond, but honestly — I didn't pick up the slightest vibe. Not like you get from the other stones once you know what to pay attention to."

"It could be slumbering," Hunter tried.

Kai looked skeptical. "If it is, then it's hibernating so deeply I couldn't feel a thing. Well, other than the slight vibe I've felt all week."

Hunter had felt it, too. A quiet pulse, a barely perceptible hum in the air. Or had he been imagining things?

"But maybe it's something totally unconnected to the Spirit Stones," Kai said.

"Like what?"

Kai shrugged. "I don't know. This resort is built on the site of an ancient temple. Maybe they pissed off some spirits or something. But I'm pretty sure that diamond is not a Spirit Stone."

"No suspicious characters sniffing around?"

Kai snorted and waved toward the party tent. "That whole slice of high society is suspicious if you ask me."

Hunter looked toward the brightly lit tent. The babble of a crowd reached out from within, and a band was warming up.

"What about that hyena shifter?"

Kai scowled. "I've had my eye on him all night. Not a sign of anything suspicious."

Hunter scowled. A hyena shifter appearing on Maui was outright suspicious as far as he was concerned, but Silas had conducted a background check and found nothing, so they'd settled for keeping close tabs on the newcomer.

"Anyway, I'm going to find Cruz and go," Kai yawned. "Got a mate to get home to, after all."

Hunter's bear nodded sadly. *I don't. Might never win her, either.*

He looked around. Dawn was somewhere near, but oh so far.

His bear cried in his mind. *Find Dawn. Maybe we can explain.*

He'd tried to explain, but he fucked up. It was time to concentrate on work. So he set one foot in front of the other and made a beeline for the bustling party tent where the rehearsal party was taking place. The moment he stepped through the entrance, his nostrils flared and his bear went from mopey to high alert.

He sniffed, scanning the faces in the room.

"Can you believe the bridesmaids' dresses?" one young woman chuckled to another.

Hunter's eyes skipped over them, trying to home in on the scent. Something not quite human, not quite shifter.

"I don't know what the designer was thinking," the young woman went on. "And Regina's dress. What was up with that?"

Hunter stepped sideways, craning his neck to check the side entrances to the tent. Who or what was making every warning bell in his body ring?

"I don't think it flatters her one bit."

He focused on a tight group of guests standing beside the bandstand. Roger Vanderpelt, the oil tycoon, was there with his usual cronies. Another man surrounded by his own entourage came striding up from a side entrance — a late arrival who made a show of shaking hands and slapping backs.

Hunter turned away, more interested in spotting the diamond ring than a businessman, but something pulled his attention back to the late arrival. Hunter craned his neck, trying to get a look at the man's face. What was it about that man that made Hunter's bear pace and grumble inside?

He kept to the edge of the tent, sidestepping chairs, chains of flowers, and two little boys creeping along to sneak up on guests. Images flooded his mind — visions that didn't fit in the least. Images of Alaska and the cabin beside the rushing creek where he'd lived as a kid. He saw his mother quilting on the porch in one of those perfect noontimes in late spring, when everything seemed new and fresh. He saw himself as a kid, throwing rocks into the river with satisfying splashes.

A dreamlike memory, but it was a nightmare, because everything had gone downhill from there.

The next image flipped into place, like a badly edited film. His mother laughed and smiled at him. But then her head whipped around to the north, and she jumped to her feet.

Hunter fisted his hands, edging closer to the elder Vanderpelts and the people clustered around them. Who was that new arrival? The big man with the silver hair?

The urgency in his mother's voice echoed through his mind. *Hunter, come to me. Quick.*

She was terrified, and though he hadn't known why at the time, he'd rushed over and hidden behind her skirt.

"You wouldn't believe how hard it is to get from Alaska to Hawaii," the big man was saying to Roger Vanderpelt as Hunter worked his way closer.

"I swear that pipeline's been twenty years in the making," Roger Vanderpelt said. "When will we finally get the paperwork lined up for it?"

Mrs. Vanderpelt sighed. "Oh, dear. That project has been giving you ulcers all these years. Do we have to talk about it now?"

"Sorry. No need to discuss business." The new arrival laughed in a low bass.

Hunter squinted, moving quickly through the glare of a light.

I'm here to discuss business, a deep voice growled in his mind. Another memory of that awful day, so long ago.

I'll never do business with you, and you know it, his mother had announced to the big man striding up to the cabin. He'd been flanked by four sidekicks, all of them grinning cruelly.

You sure about that? the man had retorted.

My mate and I told you before, and we'll tell you again— she'd started, putting her hands on her hips.

Your mate is dead, the man chuckled.

Hunter remembered his mother's knuckles going white on the backrest of the chair. He remembered squinting into the sun just like he did now against the lights in the party tent, trying to make out the face of the enemy.

Someone stepped aside, and Hunter stopped cold, seeing the face that haunted his dreams. An older, more weathered version, but the same man for sure.

Jericho Deroux, you get off my property, his mother had cried, defiant to the end.

The big man in the party tent lit a match and held up a cigar, just like he'd held a match to the pile of kindling on the cabin porch.

Don't, Hunter's mother had whispered, backing away.

"Don't," Mrs. Vanderpelt said to the guest. "No smoking, remember?"

Oh, Hunter remembered, all right. He remembered the cabin blazing away in flames. He remembered Jericho advancing as he and his mother fled toward the creek.

Run, Hunter, his mother had said in a hoarse whisper. *Run. I'll hold him off here.*

She had, too, fighting Jericho in bear form, calling upon the supernatural strength of a mother determined to protect her child. But Jericho was bigger and stronger. His knife was sharper than Hunter's mother's claws, and it sliced deeper until he finally kicked her body into the river. Hunter had paddled after her, clinging to her fur in the rushing water until they came to a stop in an eddy miles downstream. He'd spent an hour trying to nudge her back to life and another hour trembling at her side, unsure what to do. It was only when Jericho and his men came splashing down the shallows that he'd fled. Somehow, he survived two weeks in the wilds before finding a distant relative who reluctantly took him in with the strict rule that he could never, ever let his bear out. Really never, not just never-when-humans-were-around.

His hands curled into fists as his bear raged inside. That man had killed his parents in cold blood. A man who'd been reported dead — the only reason Hunter hadn't tracked him down to seek revenge.

Revenge, his bear growled. *Now.*

The points of his claws pinched the flesh under his fingernails, begging to be unleashed.

110

Jericho Deroux snuffed his match out with an annoyed shake then looked around. His nose twitched, and his eyes narrowed as he checked his surroundings.

Hunter froze as the man's eyes swept right over him on the first pass. A dozen conflicting reactions rushed through his mind.

Kill him!

Hide from him!

Lure him outside then kill him once you're out of sight.

Hunter ground his teeth. The *hiding* part stemmed from his inner cub, still lost and lonely after all these years.

No hiding. We exact our revenge, his bear growled. *Right now.*

But that wouldn't work either, not with all these humans around. Including Dawn, who had to be nearby.

Sweat broke out on his brow as he clenched his fists. Damn it all. He had to prove he wasn't the marauding beast Dawn feared. So he couldn't kill Jericho.

Not even if that monster deserves it? his bear cried.

Slowly, grudgingly, he gathered every threadbare strand of self-control and vowed not to attack Jericho.

Forgive me, mother, he whispered in his mind.

That only left him one option — to watch and wait. To figure out some way to bring Jericho down in a way Dawn wouldn't hate him for.

He stepped back into the shadows as Jericho's eyes swept the area. When the man didn't pause or show any sign of recognition, Hunter exhaled. Hybrids didn't have the keen sense of smell that shifters had, though they did possess the same raw power.

Jericho shrugged and went back to his conversation, his eyes drifting over the room, pausing on attractive young women rather than potential threats. Then his eyes darted to the entrance and blazed with renewed interest.

Hunter followed his gaze — and froze. Dawn stood there, looking gorgeous as ever. Easily the most beautiful woman at the party without even trying. Maybe the most beautiful because she *wasn't* trying. And shit — Jericho's greedy gaze grazed all over her body.

"Excuse me," Jericho murmured to the Vanderpelts and moved purposely toward Dawn, licking his lips.

Chapter Twelve

The second she'd parked the car, Dawn had hurried away from Hunter and headed for the bathroom to splash some water on her face. She needed it after the conversation she'd just had.

Mates? Battles over women? Spirit Stones? What kind of crazy world was Hunter part of?

She'd dabbed water on her neck and cheeks then headed to the party tent, frowning the whole time. For a little while, she'd thought the barriers between her and Hunter had all been knocked down. But now, they were higher than ever.

She took a deep breath and paused in the doorway to the party tent.

Time to get your head around the job, Officer Meli, she ordered herself.

The tent was packed, and a band was warming up. Not the groom's boy-toy band, thank God. More guests streamed in, some kicking grass off their shoes. Clearly, she'd made it just in time. The rehearsal over on the lawn had broken up, and everyone was starting to relax. Young men made a beeline for the buffet, while the women formed chatty huddles around the sides. Older folks and couples gathered in little batches here and there, forming their own cliques.

Her eyes swept over the scene, instinctively searching for Hunter. Where was he?

Then she caught herself and sought out the primary wedding guests instead. No more thinking of Hunter. She was undercover and on the clock, so she'd better get mingling and keep her eyes open for possible threats.

She cringed. Up until her conversation with Hunter, she'd been confident she could handle any would-be thieves. But what if a shifter battle broke out in front of her eyes? Could she handle seeing Hunter change into bear form again?

Just keep the possibility in mind, and stay safe, he'd said.

She didn't dare imagine what exactly that *possibility* might entail.

"This is nothing," one young woman sniffed to another. "My cousin got married in Tahiti. You should have seen it."

Dawn made a face. She was pretty sure she had seen that wedding in the pages of all the gossip magazines.

"Did you see Ricky?" the second woman chuckled.

Dawn looked around, but the groom was nowhere to be seen.

"I bet he's snuck off with that blonde who was throwing herself at him all day."

Dawn's eyes landed squarely on Hunter, homing in on him with some instinctive power she wasn't sure she wanted to name. He was prowling around one edge of the tent, studying the guests. No doubt keeping his eye out for the diamond, too. There were plenty to choose from, given the who's who guest list at this event. Every time he passed a woman with a low-cut top, Dawn tensed, but Hunter invariably breezed by, uninterested in the plunging necklines and surgically enhanced boobs.

Shifters believe in destined mates, he'd said. *Finding the one person who's meant for you. The one your heart is bound to forever, who you'll love to the end of your days.*

His eyes had glowed softly when he'd uttered the words. And honestly, that part of the shifter world had its appeal. It was the other aspects that worried her — the battles, the hidden enemies, the hints of a feudal society.

She watched as Hunter stepped past a woman who'd faked dropping a napkin to give Hunter a clear view down her revealing dress. Hunter seemed not to notice. His eyes and movements all centered on one guest — a big hulk of a man with silver hair and an expensive suit. Another one of the Vanderpelts' wealthy friends, she supposed.

Dawn let her eyes dart around the tent, wondering who else might be a shifter here. That tall man over by the bar — was

114

he a shifter? How about the guy laughing with a woman on either side — was he human?

Don't be silly, she decided. *Hunter is the only shifter here. Right?*

She gulped at her own question, wondering it were true. Wondering how she might tell humans apart from shifters without the latter breaking out in fur and fangs.

If she really thought about it, she remembered that Hunter had captivated her from the start. There had always been something a little different about him. His friends, too. Well, Hunter and his friends would stand out in any crowd by sheer virtue of their physiques and good looks. But there was a quiet undercurrent to each of them, too. A raw, powerful presence. And the eyes — each of them had incredibly intense eyes.

She looked back at the tall man by the bar, but his eyes were empty and bored. The man laughing with two women was more animated, but he didn't have that *blink and I just might leap over a tall building in a single bound* sense of possibility Hunter and his friends did.

"Enjoying the party?" A deep, scratchy bass sounded at her side, making her jolt.

Dawn whirled and stared at the man who'd snuck up on her. The silver-haired man she'd noticed before — a man practically as broad as he was tall, with dark, predatory eyes that seemed to swirl at hers, and a build that said he still put in plenty of hours at the gym.

She stepped back and cleared her throat. Was she enjoying the party? Not particularly, no.

"It's lovely." She forced the corners of her mouth up in a smile.

"Can I get you a drink?" he asked, touching his lapel to bring her attention to his fine, tailored suit. Was she supposed to be impressed?

"No thank you."

Her hands formed tight chopping blocks, ready to defend herself. As smooth and cultured as the man was on the surface, there was a raw, animal vibe to him, a cruel glint in his eye.

He snapped his fingers at one of the caterers. "Two champagnes."

"I said I didn't want a drink."

He grinned. "Of course you want one."

God, would she have loved to pull out her badge and tell this ass a thing or two about sexual harassment. That no meant no, regardless of how much he wanted to hear *yes*. His whole demeanor was grand and commanding. Entitled, as if she ought to react to a snap of his fingers the way the hired help might.

"You'll have to excuse me," she said, putting the emphasis on *have to* and adding a silent *asshole*.

She stepped away. As an undercover officer, she was supposed to go unnoticed, not cause a scene. And if she had to look at that jerk one minute longer, she'd be tempted to punch his arrogant face.

He grabbed her elbow — hard — and yanked her closer. "You really must try a sip." He grinned a wolfish grin, turning her stomach.

She snapped her arm upward, breaking out of his grasp. "And you really must back off. Now."

She made it an order, not a request. *It's all in the voice,* one of her first police mentors had said.

His grin turned to shock and then an angry leer that said, *I don't take orders from women. In fact, I don't take orders from anyone.*

Visions of dragging the man off in a squad car drifted through Dawn's mind, tempting her to let things escalate just so she could put the man in his place. But a good cop defused tricky situations, and she wasn't here to arrest guests.

But, shit. Hunter was prowling up behind the man, looking like a volcano about to erupt.

Thinking fast, she flashed a radiant smile and pushed past the man to take Hunter's hand. "Oh, there you are, honey," she called, pulling him away before he could make a scene. "I was looking for you."

The hair on the back of her neck rose as she sensed the tension between the two men — the older, arrogant jerk she could sense glaring, and good old, overprotective Hunter, whom she'd been trying so hard to avoid.

"Rescuing me again?" she murmured, pulling Hunter toward the dance floor. For all that she'd wanted to avoid him earlier, her body still warmed at his touch. Damn it, why did the man have such an effect on her?

She half expected Hunter to stammer some denial, but he didn't say a word. His eyes shot daggers at the older man, and his whole body bristled. His eyes glowed with anger, and the stubble on his chin seemed to thicken before her eyes. A low growl rose in his throat, and—

Oh, shit.

"Hunter," she whispered, running a hand over his shoulder.

His eyes stayed rooted on the other man, so she dragged Hunter into a turn, forcing him away. That gave her a view of the other man, and thank goodness — another guest had come up to him and started shaking his hand. A timely distraction.

Still, Hunter growled on.

"Hunter," she hissed.

His eyes snapped to hers, and. . . whoa. The sheer fury burning there made her want to back away. At the same time, she yearned to hug him tightly and make the anger go away.

She took a deep breath — deep enough for the both of them. Yes, Hunter confused the crap out of her. And, yes, the whole bear thing freaked her out. But her heart thumped with joy from being close to him, and that feeling of rightness, that sense of completion she always got around him overpowered everything else.

"Not a good time to turn into a bear," she murmured, stroking his arm.

His eyes flared before he squeezed them closed.

She went on stroking his arm, studying his tightly drawn face. So much emotion bottled up in that big man. So few outlets for it. Her touch calmed him, though. The tic on his brow softened, and his pulse slowed slightly. He tilted his head slightly toward her like a dog desperate to be petted.

"Hunter," she whispered, cupping his cheek.

117

His fingers tightened around hers, filling her with a sense of power.

"There's never a good time to turn into a bear," he murmured, sounding so wounded, she wanted to cry. The bear was part of who Hunter was, and every shackle on the bear was a shackle on Hunter's soul.

She cupped his face in both hands. "My mom used to say there's a time and place for everything."

He looked at her in surprise. "Georgia Mae used to say that, too."

Dawn nodded, remembering the eccentric old woman who'd been Hunter's guardian.

Maybe someday... she nearly said, though she bit the words back. Was she really ready to picture herself wandering the woods beside a bear? Probably not. But giving Hunter the space to do what he had to do... Maybe she could handle that.

She'd just worked her way up to a smile when a commotion broke out at one side of the tent. Dawn groaned. "Time for Regina's grand entrance, I guess."

The bride all but skipped through the crowd, and everyone turned, watching her.

"Daddy! Daddy!"

Dawn made a face. "Really, who calls their father Daddy in public?"

"Spoiled brat socialites," Hunter murmured absently. His eyes weren't on Regina, though. They were on the gray-haired man slipping out of the tent.

"Daddy, I want to see it again!"

Roger Vanderpelt shook his head for all of two seconds before Regina made a face. Then he smiled indulgently and reached into his breast pocket. The private security guards standing two steps behind him widened their stances and glared at the crowd, daring anyone to try anything.

"Well, if you insist," Roger Vanderpelt said, pulling out a jewelry box.

Everyone pressed forward as he tipped the lid open. A murmur went through the crowd as the light glinted off a gem.

"Would you look at that," someone gaped.

"That's some diamond," another whistled.

Dawn couldn't help craning her neck like everyone else. Then she glanced at Hunter, searching for some sign of recognition. What had he called it? A Spirit Stone. It had all sounded like a bunch of mumbo jumbo to her, but damn, he had been so serious. Could it really be true?

Regina held the diamond up to the light. "Isn't it something?"

On cue, guests burst into applause so painfully fawning, Dawn was embarrassed.

"Who wants to see?" Regina called out. The diamond flashed as she waved it in front of the crowd. There was a flash of purple, too, from the engagement ring on her finger.

Clearly, Regina wanted people to see *her*. The diamond was just a prop, a funnel for attention.

Regina started strutting around with the jewelry box cupped in her hands. The pair of security guards flanked her, keeping everyone back. A ripple went through the crowd as the trio made a circuit of the tent. A long, endless round in which Dawn wondered what the big deal was. But when they passed, she leaned forward in spite of herself.

The diamond glittered in the bright party tent lights, a pure, clear crystal against the black velvet of its case. Dawn glanced at Hunter. Was that a regular diamond or was it a Spirit Stone?

The reflection of the diamond lasered over his face, as did a line of purple shot out by Regina's amethyst engagement ring.

Hunter's eyes went wide, and he stood perfectly still except for his lips.

Dawn strained to hear, but she couldn't quite catch what he'd said. Was it the Spirit Stone?

Regina waved to someone with one hand, and the funny thing was, Hunter followed intently, keeping his eyes on the amethyst rather than the diamond.

But the diamond was the stone he'd mentioned, right? Dawn looked from the purple stone on Regina's finger to the diamond in her hands. Both sparkled in the brilliant lights, but the amethyst had a vibrancy to it she hadn't noticed before. And the way Hunter stared at it...

Spirit Stones... Great powers... Slumbering... Enemies... she remembered him saying.

Regina made another triumphant loop of the tent before heading back to her parents. "Where's Ricky?" she demanded, looking around for the groom. "I want him to see this, too."

"That's enough, darling. Give it back to me for safekeeping," Roger Vanderpelt said. His voice was indulgent but his hands had to twist to break the box free from Regina's grasp.

"Damn it, where is Ricky?" Regina complained.

"Watch your language, dear," her mother murmured, shooting a glance at her friends.

And off Regina went, muttering about her fiancé. Hunter's eyes followed her all the way to the door.

"Is that it? Is it a Spirt Stone?" Dawn whispered then caught herself. Wait. She didn't really believe in that kooky stuff, did she?

Hunter's lips stayed sealed for a long time, his body practically quivering with tension. He looked left and right, obviously torn between following Regina and following the gray-haired man.

"No. I mean, yes. I mean..."

"Hey," one of the buxom bridesmaids said, tapping Dawn's arm. She spoke in a conspiratorial whisper, and at first, Dawn wondered if the woman knew about the Spirit Stones. But, no.

"Your lipstick is smudged," she snipped before continuing after Regina.

Dawn stared. Did the woman think lipstick was the biggest problem she had on her hands? She rubbed the back of her hand against her mouth and turned Hunter. "Better?"

His mind was elsewhere, she could see, but he did flash a little smile. "Worse."

"Damn it." She vowed never to go undercover again. Who cared about lipstick? The problem was, if she had clown lips, she'd stick out in the crowd. Given that the Vanderpelts' private bodyguards seemed to have an eagle eye on the diamond, she figured she could dash to the restroom for one minute.

"I'll be right back," she said before moving away. And, oops— She'd been holding Hunter's hands, and her fingers slid over his as they parted, making her tingle again.

When she stepped out of the tent, the cool night air seemed fresher and cleaner than ever, at least after the stuffy party tent. Over at the main building of the resort, the line at the ladies' room stretched out into the hallway, so she turned down a side corridor to a different restroom few people used. She checked her reflection and grimaced before grabbing a paper towel to wipe the smudged lipstick away.

"Hey," someone yelped in the hallway.

Dawn went absolutely still then raced out the door. What was going on?

The next door down was a broom closet, and the door was ajar. A second later, a woman rushed out, clutching her dress. Wild-eyed, she ran past Dawn.

"Wait—" Dawn started, seeing the woman's tears and ripped resort staff uniform — the signs of a barely thwarted assault.

A man backed out of the broom closet next, and Dawn whirled, ready to tackle the man and book him.

It was Toby, the valet, and Dawn balked. Was mild-mannered Toby really capable of assaulting one of the maids?

But Toby's face was white, and his hands shook as he addressed someone else. "I won't tell. I swear. But, listen. You can't just—"

"You listen to me, kid," a bass growled from inside the closet.

Dawn stepped forward, ready to book them both, then froze as the gray-haired man emerged, jabbing a finger at Toby's chest. "You want to keep this job, you shut your—" The man broke off and jerked his head toward Dawn.

For a minute, Dawn and Toby stared at the older man like a couple of deer caught in headlights. Then the man cursed under his breath and quietly adjusted his tie — and his fly.

Dawn's heart pounded in her chest as everything fell into place. Toby hadn't committed assault. He'd inadvertently stopped one. This older man — a man Hunter had treated like a mortal enemy — had been the one to attack the young woman.

The silver-haired man strode past Dawn in a few easy steps, pausing to check his collar in a mirror before disappearing around a corner. Dawn stood, dumbstruck at his gall. She'd thought Regina was bad, but damn — this man was pure evil. Arrogant. Self-centered. A man with total disregard for anyone except himself.

"I didn't do anything," Toby said in a shaky voice. "I just opened the door, and he was..."

She hurried after the man. That monster was not getting away with this. Not on her watch.

A member of hotel security was coming her way, and she grabbed his arm, towing him along as backup.

"We need to stop that man. I'm booking him." She pointed at the back of the finely tailored suit, already heading out the front door.

"Are you nuts?" the man hissed. "You can't arrest Jericho Deroux."

Dawn froze in midstep. "Jericho..."

Jericho Deroux burned our place down, Hunter had said shortly after mentioning his mother's death.

She shook the guard's arm, needing to be sure. "Jericho who? From where?"

"Jericho Deroux. Big oil guy from Alaska. He's a close associate of the Vanderpelts. Believe me, you don't want to mess with him."

Dawn rushed out the door. Oh, but she would mess with Jericho. How many women had he assaulted in his time? How many witnesses had he threatened or bribed into silence? She ran after him, already planning her next steps. She'd grab some help and arrest the man, then track down the maid and convince her to press charges and testify. She'd personally see to it that the arrogant ass landed in jail. She'd... She'd...

She forced herself to slow down and keep cool. One little mistake, one irregularity, and the sexual assault case could be torn down by the high-end lawyers a man like Jericho was bound to have.

She peered inside the party tent. Jericho strode casually to the Vanderpelts and started chatting as if nothing had happened. Dawn felt sick, imagining his words.

Sorry I was delayed. That sweet young thing I forced into a closet refused to cooperate.

She imagined Roger Vanderpelt commiserating. *If only women kept their mouths shut and their legs spread.*

Of course, they wouldn't say any such thing. They'd talk business and politics and go on believing the world belonged to men like them.

She ground her teeth, trying to decide how to proceed. Backup, that's what she needed. She couldn't blow the case before everything was in place.

She spotted Hunter half a second after he spotted her. His tiny smile of greeting turned to a straight line of concern as she rapidly schooled her features into a calmer state. But it was too late — Hunter had spotted the look of disgust she'd shot at Jericho. His hands left his sides like a gunslinger ready to draw, and his eyes narrowed on Jericho, even angrier than before. Dawn almost wanted Hunter to turn into a bear and rip Jericho to bits. In fact, she was amazed he hadn't done so before. Jericho had killed his parents. If that wasn't proof of Hunter's self-restraint, she didn't know what was.

But Hunter had just reached his tipping point, it seemed, because he pushed away from the wall and made a beeline for Jericho.

"Oh, shit," she cursed, hurrying to intercept Hunter before it was too late.

Chapter Thirteen

The marquee bubbled with conversation, but all Hunter heard was the rush of blood in his veins. The second he'd seen Dawn walk in, looking spooked and angry — and spitting daggers at Jericho's back — he knew something had happened.

He was going to kill Jericho. He would tear the man to pieces and throw them into the sea, repercussions be damned. That man had killed his parents and burned down his home. That monster had ripped everything he cherished out of his life. And now, Jericho had done something to spook Dawn. How could Hunter not exact revenge?

He'd exercised self-restraint the first time Jericho provoked him. There wouldn't be a second time. He'd had enough.

"Wait, Hunter. Don't," Dawn urged, catching his arm.

He nearly pulled free, but just like before, her touch sent a soothing wave of goodness through him, and his rage ebbed away. Not far — the fury was still there, simmering beneath the surface — but at least it ceased pushing steam out of his ears.

"Hunter, listen to me. I have a better idea," Dawn said.

A better idea implied that she'd considered killing Jericho, too, and that was enough to stop him in his tracks. Dawn — his Dawn — was capable of that much hate?

Her eyes met his, and he saw his fury mirrored. Fury and determination, along with the faint outlines of a plan.

And, hell. A smart woman's plan was always better than a raging bear's vague notions of revenge. So he followed Dawn to the side door and out into the fresh air.

Dawn shot a look back at Jericho as Hunter took her hands. They were shaking the slightest bit — from anger, not fear.

She'd make a great bear, his inner beast murmured.

He held back his *Amen.* Much as he liked the idea, the only thing more volatile than one vengeful bear was two, especially at a time like this.

"What happened?" He touched her hair, her shoulder. "Did he lay a hand on you? Did he hurt you?"

Dawn shook her head vehemently. "I swear that man would be rolling on the floor cradling his crushed balls if he'd tried."

Hunter winced — and glowed with pride at the same time. His mate had come a long way since her high school days. But Jericho was a hybrid, and there was no way Dawn could fight Jericho off once he unleashed his full powers.

"He went at one of the maids. Toby stumbled across them, thank God."

Hunter made a mental note to let the kid drive the Rolls around the resort grounds when things finally settled down — if things ever settled down. He had the sinking feeling it would be a hell of a night.

Kai! Cruz! he shouted across the mental connection they'd developed over the years. He needed backup, and soon. Jericho added a whole new level of danger to the situation — that, and the fact that they might have a Spirit Stone on their hands after all.

"I nearly booked Jericho, but I realized it would be better to do it quietly," Dawn went on.

Hunter's inner bear nodded vigorously. *Quiet. Right. We drag Jericho out into the shadows and tear him apart where no one can see. Quietly. And* then *Dawn can book him.*

"So I thought—"

A scream cut Dawn off, and they both snapped their heads toward the beach.

"No!" a woman cried.

"Now what?" he muttered.

Dawn sprinted toward the cry half a second before Hunter did. A few steps later, she stopped to pull off her shoes before running onward, barefoot.

"Dawn, wait!" he cried, following her. What the hell was happening now? Was another woman being attacked?

The cries continued, a whole barrage of words, protests, and — insults? — all coming from the beach. Past the yellow tape and the signs that said, *Warning! High surf. Beach closed until further notice.* Hunter crested the rise and slowed when he saw who it was.

Regina, throwing the mother of all hissy fits, and with good reason for a change.

"You little shit! You asshole!" she cried, kicking sand at a couple crouched in the sand.

"Regina, I can explain," Ricky, the groom, protested.

Hunter almost felt for the guy. Almost, but not quite, because Ricky was naked, and so was the girl he was with. What kind of lowlife cheated on his fiancée on the eve of his own wedding?

"And you!" Regina screeched at the buxom blonde. "I thought you were my friend, you slut!"

Waves pounded the shoreline behind them — big, twenty-five-footers unusual for this leeward shore.

"We were just... Uh..." Ricky tried.

Hunter turned around and started walking back the way he'd come. He didn't have time for this shit.

"You were just screwing my bridesmaid, you shit!"

That Regina — she sure had a way with words. Hunter shook his head, then turned to see if Dawn was following — just in time to see Regina yank her engagement ring off her finger and wind her arm back for a throw.

"Wait," Hunter shouted, rushing toward her. If the amethyst was what he thought it was...

"We're over. You're over, Ricky. I'll have Daddy kill your career."

"Regina, baby," Ricky tried. But it was too late.

Regina's arm snapped forward — a damn good throw, right down to the wrist snap; Hunter had to give her that — and the amethyst went flying. Time slowed as Hunter watched it arc through the air. A flashing purple line marked its path as it glittered in the moonlight — like a meteor, streaking across the night sky, glowing the whole way.

Make that, streaking toward the ocean where the waves gnashed their teeth.

"You crazy bitch!" Ricky yelled. "You know what that ring is worth?"

Hunter's jaw swung open, his eyes glued to the supernatural glow. That ring was worth more than any human could imagine, because only a Spirit Stone glowed like that.

He reached into thin air as if to will it back. Holy shit. Kai was right — the diamond wasn't a Spirit Stone. But the amethyst was. Hunter hadn't been entirely sure before, but now he knew. The stone called to him like a magnet. He'd sensed its power when Regina had paraded her wedding ring around the tent.

Why hadn't he sensed it earlier? Because the damn thing had been slumbering, he figured, until proximity to the diamond roused its powers.

Gems are like jealous women, Silas had once explained. *At least, that's what my grandfather used to say.*

The amethyst emitted a last pulse of bright purple light then sliced into the raging sea and disappeared.

Hunter ran toward the pounding surf, then stopped short. An invisible wall went up in front of him, and a slew of ugly memories rushed through his head. Memories of rushing water, trying to drag him under as he fought desperately to stay with his mother. The sting of salt in his eyes and throat. The bash of boulders beneath the surface. The desperate clawing motion that got him nowhere through the rushing estuary where the river met the sea.

Mom, the cub in him cried. *No. No. Please...*

He stood, rooted to the spot, facing his single greatest fear.

Then something rushed by his side and splashed through the shallows. Dawn. His Dawn, rushing in after the Spirit Stone, totally unfazed.

"No!" he shouted. God, no. The stone wasn't worth it. Not even a Spirit Stone. Not with a freak offshore storm kicking the surf to record heights and churning the water into lethal undercurrents.

But Dawn dove in with the grace of a native-born island girl who'd grown up with the Pacific as her playground.

"Dawn!" he yelled, yanking his jacket off.

How she planned to swim in that tight dress, he had no clue. And how he would ever force himself into the water given all the ghosts in his head — shit, he *really* had no clue. But he ripped off his shirt and plowed in after Dawn nonetheless.

Water. Bad water, something deep in his soul screamed as spray pelted his face.

Mate! Must help my mate! his bear roared even louder.

"Dawn!" he yelled, forcing himself forward in the brief lull between two waves. Didn't Dawn know this was crazy? And, shit — she'd dived right under a breaking wave to swim out, but she hadn't come up again.

Mate, his bear cried desperately. *Mate.*

He might as well have thrown open the door to a haunted house full of rotting, moaning zombies — it was that bad, that bone-achingly wrong. But his mate was in there. In danger. Alone.

Hunter took the deepest breath of his life and dove in, only to be tumbled back by a massive wave.

Panic rose in his veins. *Dawn! Dawn!*

He'd been in a dozen hellish situations in his active service days — certain death situations with deafening explosions that had rattled his bones and his faith in the world. And he'd kept a cool head every time. But this time, his mate's life was at stake, and that shook him to the core.

It won't help Dawn if you don't keep a clear head, he yelled at his bear.

He timed his next attempt more carefully and dove under the wave instead of into it. The force of rushing water pulled at his pants, but the undercurrent sucked him out to sea instead of tossing him back onto the beach. He kicked forward, keeping his eyes wide despite the salty sting. Water flooded his ears and his mouth as he formed bubbly underwater shouts.

Dawn! Dawn!

An eternity later, he popped up for a breath of air — beyond the breakers, thank goodness — and looked around.

"Dawn!"

Nothing. An eerie, swirling nothing made all the more terrifying by the night.

Something splashed to his left, and he whipped around. "Dawn!"

She came up ten strokes away and immediately dove again, too quickly to hear his anguished cry.

Dive, he ordered himself. *Go.*

He might as well have told an arachnophobe to stick a hand in a jar of hairy tarantulas, and yet Hunter dove. Not for the damn gem. For Dawn. For his mate.

The water rolled and roiled, tugging him downward, spinning him around. Little streaks of bioluminescence flashed merrily, as if this were all a game. He kicked with all his might, finding nothing, then popped up again.

Panting, he found himself a good fifty yards from where he had entered the water — the current was that strong. He had to get Dawn and get the hell out of the water before it sapped their last reserves.

"We have to get back," he yelled, seeing Dawn come up sputtering a few yards away.

She shook her head vehemently and clawed at her shoulders as if peeling a clingy octopus away.

Her dress, he realized. She was ripping her dress off to free her arms and legs.

"You said it's important, right?" she growled, wrestling with the fabric.

Hunter paddled closer, wondering if he dared lie. *Um, no. I made a mistake. It's not the Spirit Stone, so let's just swim back to shore and forget about it, okay?*

"You said in the hands of the enemy it could be used for harm. Right?" She went on.

This pep talk, he didn't need. Not with wave after wave lifting and dropping them both before rolling onward.

"And since Jericho is the enemy..." she added, looking fiercer than ever.

Hunter wanted to scream. Jericho was his enemy, not Dawn's. How had he ever dragged her into all this?

130

"It's the amethyst, not the diamond. Right?" she yelled.

Dawn didn't wait for an answer, but his expression must have given it away. She dove, graceful as a dolphin, the moonlight kissing her bare skin.

Hunter stared for a moment, dying to protest. *Your aumakua is an owl, not a dolphin, so let's get the hell out of here.*

"Damn it." He gulped a lungful of air and followed as Dawn plunged into the inky depths.

It was eerie as hell, what with the water dampening all noise and darkness closing in — the soul-sucking darkness of the sea at midnight. Moonlight only pierced a few feet beyond the frothy surface. Everything beyond it an abyss.

"This is nuts," he yelled the next time they surfaced, already calculating how to grab Dawn and tow her back to land, with or without her consent.

"I saw the ring! The current has been pushing it along, but it's right there. It's so close!" Her eyes shone and, with a nimble splash of the feet, she dove again.

Dawn dove like a seabird; Hunter submerged with all the grace of a rusty submarine. Red alarms buzzed through every nerve in his body. *A-woo-ga! A-woo-ga!*

He was never, ever going to touch salt water again. He might just swear off showers, too, if he and Dawn somehow survived this nightmare. They'd been swept out even farther, and the sea was choppy and raw. How could she possibly have seen the amethyst?

He kicked into the depths, following the pale flash of her feet. Frustrated as hell and, yes — scared, too. But then something flashed, catching his eye.

A purple flash from the indigo depths. The Spirit Stone?

Of course it's the Spirit Stone, his bear retorted. *Grab it and get this over with.*

He kicked deeper, chasing the stone — and Dawn. The pressure in his ears doubled until he thought his head would explode. Dawn was a full body length deeper than him. How the hell did she do it?

The amethyst called to him as the current tumbled it along.

Follow me. Come to me. You need my help, the purple glow seemed to say.

Hunter gritted his teeth. He didn't need a goddamn stone. He needed his mate.

You need me to protect her. The purple light wobbled through the underwater eddies.

He snorted and immediately choked on salt water. How the hell was the amethyst — the Earthstone — going to protect his mate out in the sea? On the contrary, it was endangering her, luring her into treacherous waters.

The purple light pulsed. *You need me.*

Hunter kicked back to the surface and sputtered for air, looking around desperately for Dawn.

A moment later, she breached out of the sea like a porpoise showing off its next trick.

"I nearly had it!"

He grabbed for her hand but missed. "Leave it, Dawn. We have to leave it."

"I can get it! I'm sure I can."

Famous last words, he was sure of it.

"The current is too strong." He waved at the shoreline. Soon, they'd be swept around the corner and then — dashed against rocks? Dragged out to the open sea? Drowned by the undertow swirling around his ankles?

"Trust me," she said, diving again.

Hunter stared at the splash in her wake. She wanted him to trust her with something as crazy as this?

"Wait—" he started, then stopped cold.

Trust me.

He'd asked her to take a much bigger leap of faith in trusting him — the man she'd witnessed transforming out of grizzly form. He treaded water for one stunned moment then took a deep breath and dove. Although instinct told him to grab Dawn's ankle and abandon the amethyst, he followed his mate. Quick as a fish, Dawn swam down, kicking smoothly against the current. The Spirit Stone glowed from the depths, calling to him.

You need me. She needs me.

Hunter's head spun, but down he went. For Dawn, not for the jewel. Only for his mate.

Trust me, the gem murmured. Or were those Dawn's words echoing in his cloudy mind?

The water pressure pounded inside his head. He squinted, trying to keep the world in focus when it was blurring rapidly. One second, the Spirit Stone was there, winking at him, and the next, it was gone.

Hunter contorted through a spin. Damn it. He'd been so close. Dawn had been, too. Where the hell was the stone?

The invisible hand of the sea spun him around and around until he couldn't tell up from down any more. His lungs ached as he clawed wildly.

Drowning. He was drowning.

But he couldn't drown. Not until he got Dawn to safety, at least.

He searched desperately for some underwater landmark or the glow of the Earthstone, but there was nothing. Just a watery abyss. His vision dimmed, and he started imagining things. Like a mermaid swimming by and grabbing his hand. He pushed the mermaid away. Where was Dawn?

Hunter, her voice sounded faintly in his mind as bubbles streamed out of the mermaid's mouth.

He blinked his raw eyes. Whoa. That wasn't a mermaid. It was Dawn, and she was motioning to him. A second later, they both shot upward and broke through the surface, gasping for air.

"I got it!" she cried, holding up a tightly curled fist. Between her fingers, purple light glowed, reflecting in her eyes and her radiant face. "I got the ring!"

Hunter took hold of her arm. This time, he was not letting her go. Between gasps, he yelled. "You are crazy, you know that?"

She laughed. "Crazier than a guy who can turn into a bear?"

"Definitely crazier."

And in spite of everything, his bear sighed dreamily. *Definitely mine.*

133

"Let's get out of here," she said, pointing — not to the beach, but to the rocky promontory that stretched into the sea.

Hunter looked at her askance. Had she swallowed too much salt water? Or maybe she really was a mermaid...

"If we go back, we fight the current. If we go that way, we can ride it."

"Sure. Ride it right out to Lanai," he warned, indicating the island ten miles away.

She shook her head, treading water lightly. "We just have to break out at the right moment when we get around the turn. Come on, Hunter. Where we you all the times we kids went swimming around Sandy Point?"

He'd been cowering somewhere with his tail between his legs, thinking of his mother, damn it.

"It's exactly the same," Dawn said. "Trust me."

There it was again — trust. Five little letters that were at the crux of the issues that divided him and his mate. It wasn't so much about shifters and humans, or the divide between women and men. It all came down to trust. If he wanted her to trust him, he had to trust her.

Hunter paddled closer to her side and forced himself to nod. "Okay."

Dawn had made it sound easy, but her facial muscles tightened when they swept out and around the point where the surf crashed high against the rocks. They bobbed along just outside the frothy strip, waiting for their chance.

"Now?" he asked — nearly begged — as the first sliver of beach appeared on the other side of the point.

"Not yet," she murmured, judging some unseen factors Hunter couldn't begin to fathom. A good thing his island beauty had been a water baby all her life.

"Now?" he tried again, eyeing the rocks they swept past.

She shook her head, but a second later, she yelped and swam hard. "Now!"

Hunter rushed after her, kicking to break free of the strangling undercurrent. Water swirled around his shoulders and legs, trying to convince him to stay out and play.

To stay out and die was more like it. He swam onward until he nearly collided with Dawn, who had paused.

"Now what?" he panted.

"Now we just ride the surf in," she said.

Just and *surf* were two words that combined about as well as *fun* and *explosives*, at least as far as Hunter was concerned. Especially with the surf this high. Dawn treaded water with one hand closed tight around the Spirit Stone and studied the waves the way a surfer did.

"Next one's ours."

From the looks of it, getting out of the water would be as hard as getting in had been, given the way the waves pounded into the shore.

"Here we go," Dawn muttered, paddling slowly forward. She accelerated as the wave rose, lifting them higher.

Hunter did his best to clear his mind and followed. All he had to do was endure this one last part. Then he — and more importantly, Dawn — would be home free.

The water lifted him, building into a massive wave. There was a certain rush to it, a handing-over-of-control to the elements. But the water rose higher and higher, taking him with it until he was peering down the lip of a towering cliff. The water gurgled, rushed, and then roared as the wave broke.

Hunter went from riding the crest to plummeting into an abyss, where he was sucked under. He tumbled around and around, clawing at the water like a man in a spin cycle, desperate to find the way out.

The earsplitting roar became a quieter hiss, and just like that, he ground against the shallows. He stood just in time to be bowled over by the next wave. It tugged at his feet, trying to pull him back to the sea. But he was in now, and Dawn was, too — beaching herself just the way kids did. He stumbled over and found her panting and wild-eyed.

"Okay," she murmured, accepting a hand up. "That was exciting."

Exciting? Hunter hauled her up a safe distance from the waves and trapped her in a giant hug. Exciting was early spring in Alaska, when the meadows came alive with wildflowers, bees, and sunshine. Exciting was the way his heart rate tripled every time he looked at Dawn. Exciting was the idea of her hugging him without the slightest sense of reservation, as if she believed as firmly in destined mates as he did.

Just as she did right then.

Heaven. Hunter found himself transported from sheer hell to heaven. He touched her back, her waist, her hair, assuring himself she was all right. He breathed her in along with the scent of strawberry guava, wafting over from shore.

"Hunter," she murmured.

He didn't move. He couldn't move.

"Hunter." She tapped his back.

"Hmm?" he mumbled into her hair.

"Don't you want to see the gem?" Dawn asked, her voice muffled at his shoulder.

He blinked, confused. Oh, right. The Spirit Stone.

Nah, his bear breathed, and his human side agreed.

"Need another second with you," he murmured. A flat-out lie because he'd need at least a week to catch his breath after what had just happened. Preferably, a week spent this close to his mate.

"Hey," she whispered. "I'm okay."

He sure as hell wasn't. Not yet, anyway.

Other than the sound of the surf hammering the shore, the beach was peaceful. No screaming brides, no blaring music, no crowds. Just him and his mate under a thousand twinkling stars. Alive. They'd come ashore on the far side of the resort, and no one was around.

He pulled back at last and held her by the shoulders.

"Nice, huh?" she whispered, holding up the amethyst.

He kept his eyes glued on hers. "Gorgeous." Slowly, his eyes drifted over her soaked bra and panties, and all the skin in between.

There was a painting he'd seen in an art book at some point — a painting of Venus coming out of the water. It was supposed to embody feminine beauty, but Hunter knew better. Dawn had that goddess beat, easy.

She looked at the amethyst. "So, a Spirit Stone. Is that why it glows?"

He nodded. Not that he was an expert on the jewels — hell, even Silas, who'd researched every scrap of dragon lore for information on the Spirit Stones, didn't know the whole story — but, yeah. Normal jewels didn't glow like that. That much, he knew.

She tipped the amethyst from her hands into his. "Here, you take it."

He tipped it right back. "No, you."

A twig snapped behind them, and a deep voice snickered. "How about I take it?"

Hunter whirled, pushing Dawn behind his body.

"Jericho," he spat, shaking with fury.

"So good of you to retrieve the Spirit Stone for me. And I see you've brought me a further gift." Jericho smirked, letting his eyes run over Dawn's near-naked body.

Six hulking figures crept up to flank Jericho. Hunter flexed his fingers, letting his claws push painfully close to the surface.

"Over my dead body," he growled.

Jericho chuckled. "Yes. That's exactly my plan."

Chapter Fourteen

For one brief instant when she'd first stepped foot on the beach, Dawn had been jubilant. She'd done it! She'd ridden the eddies and escaped the current with the amethyst. She'd made it back to shore unscathed, and Hunter had given her the hug of her life.

So, really, it was time to do a little victory dance, right?

But then Jericho Deroux had turned up and made her blood run cold.

As a police officer, Dawn had been in more than one close-call situation in her life. Even Maui had its dark, criminal side, and she'd seen it all. But she'd never, ever sensed anything like the brutally evil vibes coming off the man on the beach.

Jericho had murdered in cold blood before; she was sure of it. And he would do it again. He would eliminate any man who stood in his way and take any woman who whetted his appetite.

A cool, calculating compartment of her mind started running through police procedures for dealing with this kind of psychopath. But none of that would work now, and she knew it.

Hunter stood taller and broader than she'd ever seen him, shielding her near-naked body with his. Normally, she'd roll her eyes and claim her own space, but these were shifters, and normal rules didn't apply. That much was obvious. The question was, what rules did apply?

Feudal laws, her gut told her. *Fight for your life.*

"Give me the Spirit Stone." Jericho snapped his fingers.

Hunter glanced at Dawn. Sometimes, the man was impossible to read. But now, he was an open book — looking at her,

139

then the ring, then at Jericho. Weighing up if he could trade the ring for her life.

Dawn's mouth cracked open. Hunter had gone on and on about how important the Spirit Stones were and how critical it was to keep them out of enemy hands. Was he really considering giving one up for her sake?

The man was a prince. Her prince, even if he was part bear.

No, she let her eyes say. *That lowlife would never honor an agreement anyway.*

She tightened her fingers around the ring and glared at Jericho.

Hunter snarled under his breath. His teeth were bared, his hands balled into fists, and he was practically shaking with rage — but he was holding back.

For her. He was holding back for her. If she were facing her mother's murderer, would she have the same restraint?

"The ring," Jericho barked.

"Oh, you mean this ring?" she said coolly, stepping into view and making a show of slipping it on her finger. "I don't think so."

The second she worked the ring past the second joint of her ring finger, a little surge went through her. A purple glow kindled in the heart of the stone, and her hand warmed. Whoa — was that a good or a bad sign?

Jericho scowled. "You don't know who you're messing with, baby."

You're the one who doesn't know who you're messing with, asshole. Years of police work helped her hold back the words, but she let her eyes telegraph them. Jericho might be rich, powerful, and dangerous, but if he thought she'd be a soft target, he'd better think again.

Hunter made a subtle gesture with his elbow, hinting for her to sneak away, but she stood firm at his side.

"I said, give me that ring," Jericho snarled.

Dawn glanced around, considering her options. This corner of the resort was deserted, and the noise of the rehearsal party would drown out any call for help. The sea was at her back, and the high, rocky point she and Hunter had swum around was at her left. The beach stretched away to her right until it ended in another point of the coast and made a hard turn out of sight.

"Is Cruz around?" she whispered to Hunter. "Or Kai?" She'd been avoiding his shifter friends all week, but heck, she wouldn't mind seeing them now.

Hunter gave a terse shake of his head. It was just the two of them, alone.

She looked around for a makeshift weapon. A piece of driftwood, perhaps, or a discarded bottle. Anything.

Her finger throbbed as if the ring were trying to tell her something, and a winged form swooped through the sky, heading for Jericho. The big man swiped at it as it flew past.

"Goddamn bat."

Hunter used the distraction to whisper in warning. "These guys are shifters. Shifters and... worse."

She looked at the hulking men on the beach. What was worse than a shifter? Several of the men had Hunter's bulky build, so maybe those were bears. One of the others was leaner and lithe, reminding her of Cruz. God, what if he was a tiger? The others were somewhere in between, and Jericho — she would have pegged him as a bear, but now — well, she wasn't so sure.

"I'm sorry I got you into this," Hunter murmured.

She shook her head. "*We* got into this. We'll get out."

"We'll?" Hunter's voice rose in hope.

She nodded, not trusting her voice just then. The secret world of shifters was still a lot to swallow, but Hunter? The man was a keeper, bear or no bear.

"I love you, Hunter. I trust you," she said.

She could have spent an hour gazing into the eyes that looked at her in gratitude and relief, but all she had time for was a quick glance before Jericho sneered.

"Hunter? Now, where do I know that name from? Let me see." He made a show out of stroking his chin. "Oh, that's right. The cowardly little cub who turned tail and fled all those years ago."

Hunter stiffened, but Dawn sneered back. "Let me guess. You outnumbered his family ten-to-one?"

Jericho's eyes narrowed on her. "A little like we outnumber you now, my dear."

Dawn tried telling herself seven-to-two wasn't so bad.

"What a tough guy you are," she retorted, dripping sarcasm.

Jericho seemed not to hear. "Lucky for you, a man in my position doesn't have to share his prize. I'll have you all to myself."

Her stomach turned.

Jericho gestured, motioning his henchmen forward.

Hunter's hand tightened on her arm as three of the men advanced. One pulled at his collar. Another unbuttoned his jacket and tossed it aside. A third made a garbled noise and doubled over as the others chuckled in anticipation.

"Bears," Hunter grunted in her ear, preparing her. "Two bears and a wolf."

They hunched and ripped right out of their clothes, landing on all fours in grotesque, twisted forms. Each made choked, snarling sounds as fur sprouted along their bare backs and their muzzles stretched.

Wings fluttered overhead — the bat making a second pass — and Jericho muttered again.

Please. No vampires, Dawn wanted to beg, keeping her eyes on the men transforming into animals before her very eyes.

The process wasn't instantaneous, but it didn't take long either. The wolf was the first to take full form. It snorted, gave its gray coat a hard shake, then stalked toward her slowly, swishing its tail. The bears lumbered forward a moment later, grumbling under their breath. The men left standing behind them snickered and looked on.

"Dawn," Hunter murmured.

Dawn forced herself to nod. "Do it. Shift."

She faked a strong, sure voice, but inside, she was quaking. She looked around, studiously avoiding Hunter and the soft grunts he made. She and Hunter stood a better chance if he shifted. And, damn it, she needed to get ready to fight, too.

142

A piece of driftwood bobbed in the water to her left, and she grabbed it. A solid, four-foot length she could heft like a club. She took a test swing and nearly jumped back from the sheer force of it slamming into the ground.

Whoa. Had she just done that?

The ring tightened on her finger and glowed brighter. At the same time, something big and wet moved at her side. She turned back, gaping at the grizzly at her side. A huge, hulking beast that shook its thick coat and looked at her with soulful eyes.

"Hunter," she whispered. Holy shit.

She'd recognize the eyes anywhere, even if the rest was a shock. His twitching black nose. His thick, chocolate-brown coat. His stub of a tail.

"Hunter." She shook her head, awestruck.

He chuffed and swung his nose toward her hand.

Please, his eyes seemed to beg. *Please accept me.*

Dawn took a deep breath. There were times in life where you rushed through a make-or-break moment without even recognizing it, but this simple gesture — touching Hunter — was a slow-motion, stay-in-your-heart-forever kind of thing. A crossroads at which a second became a full minute, at least in her mind.

She flexed her fingers and inched her hand forward until they touched. Fingers to snout. Human to bear. One lover to another.

Oh. My. God.

His nose was cool, like a dog's, and the puff of his breath warm. It came out as a sigh of relief, and his eyes sparkled.

"Hunter," she whispered.

He nosed closer, stopping at the ring, then glancing at her.

Right. The ring. The Spirit Stone. The one with magical powers.

Never in her life had she been as tempted to grab a wild animal's snout and shake some words out. *What do I do with it? How does it work?*

Then a wolf growled, and Hunter jerked away. He stalked up the beach, leaving dinner-plate-sized tracks in the sand as he cut off Jericho's men.

Dawn had just enough time to lift the driftwood to her shoulder and suck in a long breath before the fight broke out.

"Hurry up, already," Jericho said, sounding bored. "Kill him. Her, I want alive."

The low snarls broke into outright roars as the shifters launched into an attack. The wolf came at her while the bears rammed into Hunter with a thump she could feel in her bones.

"Hunter!" Dawn cried, swinging the wood to fend off the wolf. It jumped back, then darted forward, snapping at her feet.

The bears slashed and clawed at each other, peeling their lips back to bare huge teeth. Hunter reared on his hind legs, swiped one opponent, and tackled the other. They rolled in a blur of fur and fangs.

Dawn swung the wood at the wolf. It was driving her back, opening a gap between her and Hunter. Driving her toward—

She whirled just in time to duck away from one of Jericho's men who was sneaking up from behind.

"I said, get her!" Jericho yelled from his vantage point.

Every time the man spoke, the anger in her bubbled higher, and the amethyst glowed brighter.

"Take that." She smacked the wolf on the shoulder so hard, she lost her grip on the driftwood. Still, the beast yelped and rolled away.

Somewhere in the back of Dawn's mind, it registered that there was something strange about that. The beast was a good 250 pounds, and yet she'd made it roll at least ten feet. But she didn't have time to think because the man was back, grabbing at her again.

She wound back for a punch and threw it with all her might. The way she did every Friday at the gym, imagining the man who'd tried to rape her. Which made for a pretty powerful punch that channeled all the power in her body.

But, damn. This punch landed with a crack and sent the man tumbling backward until his ass hit the sand.

Dawn gaped at her own fist. Even at her fiercest, she'd never moved the punching bag the way her male colleagues did. But, heck — that punch had enough power in it to rip a punching bag right off its chains.

She took a deep, shaky breath, staring at the ring. The amethyst set in the middle glowed — smugly, almost.

A bear roared, dragging her attention to the right, where the wolf was springing at her again. She diverted it with a vicious kick. The beast rolled to its feet and eyed her, panting. The way its tongue hung out of its mouth said, *Holy shit.*

Holy shit was right. Dawn flexed her fingers. How much power did that stone contain? And how long might it help her fight off these crooks?

Chapter Fifteen

When a bear screamed in pain, Dawn winced, praying it wasn't Hunter. She whirled around. The two grizzlies he faced were each slightly smaller, but they outnumbered him, and who knew when their buddies would join in to help. She glanced at the ring, willing it to present her with some way to fight a creature as big as a bear. Even if it did augment her physical strength, it wouldn't make her sprout fangs or claws.

She gulped. *God, I hope not.*

"You and you. Get down there," Jericho ordered the other men. "I want him dead. Now! And I want her in one piece."

The three men stalked forward, and Dawn despaired. Even if she and Hunter could hold them off for a time, there was no way to escape so many foes.

One thing at a time, she decided, backing up. The man she'd punched made a choked sound, and she wondered if she'd broken his nose. But when she glanced over, she spotted a cougar, not a man. Its yellow-brown eyes shone the way a cat's did when it prepared to pounce, and its shoulders hunched.

She grabbed the driftwood and brandished it. "Try me," she dared them. "Just try me."

The cougar growled as if it couldn't wait to sink those fangs into her neck. The beast was on her in a flash, knocking her to the ground. She rolled, and the cougar rolled with her, snapping at her with its huge canines. She shoved it with another supernatural burst of power and scrambled away, but the furious animal sprang right back, looming over her.

"I want her alive!" Jericho yelled.

The cougar gnashed its teeth, obviously more interested in revenge than the boss's orders. It pounced, and she threw up her hands. "No!"

Hunter roared, but he was too far, too busy with his own foes to help.

The air over her body whooshed, and she braced for the tearing impact of the massive feline. But all she felt was a light flutter. The flutter of wings.

She opened her eyes and scuttled backward like a crab.

"*Pu'eo,*" she breathed.

That hadn't been a bat that had flown past Jericho before. It was an owl. An owl aiming its talons at the cougar and fluttering frantically around the feline's eyes, giving Dawn time to escape. She jumped to her feet and stared in shock.

She'd never had reason to question the stories that had been passed down through generations — stories that insisted that their ancestral spirits took the shapes of owls. But she'd assumed there was a tall-tale element to *aumakua* legends, too.

Apparently not.

The owl was only a big as her forearm — nowhere near as big as the shifters around them — but it fought with ferocious determination.

Go, its frantic wingbeats signaled. *Get away.*

Hunter roared, and she wavered, torn between running for help or staying at his side. But then the wolf came at her, too, and its teeth clacked an inch away from her face. With one swift kick, she pushed free and ran down the beach. Enough was enough. Her only option was to run for help.

Footsteps pounded behind her, and Jericho yelled.

"Damn it. You finish off the bear. You and you, help me catch her."

Dawn gasped, spotting a new arrival sprinting at her from the opposite direction. Another of Jericho's shifters?

She threw an arm up and ducked when the oncoming beast jumped.

"What the..." she muttered when it sailed right over her, intent on some other target. She watched the orange and black blur in confusion. A tiger?

Hunter roared behind her. A glad roar, if there was such a thing, with a distinct note of *Thank God you're here.*

"Cruz," she whispered, staring as the tiger entered the fray.

Hunter's bear was a mammoth, crushing everything in sight, while Cruz's nimble tiger leaped this way and that with the spectacular moves of an acrobat. The wolf screamed in agony; the cougar hissed and backed away.

Dawn wanted to cheer. Cruz had just tipped the odds from impossible to really, really unlikely, and she'd take what she could get.

The only man — or beast — not locked in battle was Jericho, and his eyes narrowed on her.

"You," he growled, advancing again.

Dawn was sorely tempted to try the Spirit Stone's power on Jericho, but her better sense prevailed, and she ran. Her bare feet slipped in the sand then thumped over the prickly grass as she headed away from the beach.

The owl swooped overhead then whooshed right over her, intent on Jericho.

"Damn it," the man yelled.

Dawn glanced back, seeing him falter then grope around for a stone to bash the owl with.

"No!" she cried as he hefted a wrecking-ball-sized boulder off the ground.

With a mighty grunt, he threw the boulder at the owl, who beat a hasty retreat. Dawn stared at the distance the boulder covered. It landed with a solid thump.

"I said, I want that ring," Jericho growled, coming after her.

Dawn ran, wondering what kind of shifter he was — or whether he was a shifter at all. Maybe Jericho was just a man with superhuman strength. She frowned, imagining what a man like him might do with the power of the Spirit Stone.

The Earthstone, Hunter had called it. Her mind spun, trying to puzzle out what that implied.

She was about to crest the rise that led to the main section of the resort when a hunched dog — no, a hyena — appeared out of nowhere, baring an uneven row of teeth. It cut her off, and with Jericho barreling up from behind, she only had one choice — to race up the rocky promontory she and Hunter had swum around. The same promontory she'd stood on earlier when Regina had come by.

She hesitated at the sign that said, *Pass at your own risk.* The cliff wasn't only unstable — it was a dead end, too. What was she going to do when she reached the top?

Somewhere behind her, the hyena yelped, and a feline growl split the night. She prayed that was Cruz. Paws scraped the earth as the shifter battle waged on. Human feet hammered along, too, and Jericho stormed up behind her.

Dawn stumbled and clawed at the ground with her hands and feet until she reached the very top. She peered over the sheer drop, hoping she might be able to dive into the sea. But the cliff ended in jagged rocks — instant death. Which had some appeal, given the alternative Jericho had in mind.

She turned, bringing her one foot back and her hands up in a defensive position. Would jujitsu work against a man like Jericho?

He slowed to a walk then stopped in front of her, yanking a huge knife from his boot. His eyes glowed red — blood red, like a ghoul — and he chuckled. "Now what will you do, eh?"

Dawn gritted her teeth. She was wondering the same thing.

"I'll tell you what you will do," he went on, dropping his voice to an ugly threat. "First, you take the ring off before I cut it off."

Dawn refused to imagine the details of that.

"Then you get down on your knees..." His face twisted into a smile. "And you follow my instructions very carefully."

She wondered whether his instructions might involve stepping off the cliff or sucking his dick. Both sickened her, but she'd take the cliff in a heartbeat.

She flexed her fingers, wishing the ring could conjure up a miraculous solution for her. A light saber, maybe. A battle ax. Anything to take this man down.

But the Spirit Stone didn't do a thing but glow.

Help me, she wanted to yell as she shook it. *Help, please.*

Jericho smiled. "Silly human. The Earthstone might enhance your powers to a degree — but it will multiply my power exponentially." His eyes shone in greed as he reached forward.

"And you'll do what with that power?"

Jericho scoffed, and she hated him that much more. "I'll do what I always do. Create wealth and let it trickle down. Spread prosperity."

"So it's all for the general good. Sure. Right."

He laughed. "There are always a few who fail to see the light. Tree huggers. Those damn flower power types." He put air quotes around the term.

"Hunter's parents," she added to his list.

Jericho shrugged. "Misguided fools. They had their chance to cash in. No one can stop me — least of all you. Now give me that stone."

She wavered one more second, then raised her hand. "Fine," she snapped. "Take it."

His eyes glittered like moonlight over a blood-red sea, and he stepped closer. "Good girl. Maybe I won't be too rough the first time I try you out."

Bile rose in her throat, but she kept her hand steady, letting the purple glow lure him on.

"I've searched for this for so long," he muttered.

Paws scratched the earth lower down in the hill, and every muscle in Dawn's body tensed. Were more shifters approaching? If so, which?

"Mine," Jericho murmured, leaning over the ring.

Dawn forced herself to wait before executing her last-ditch plan. "Yours," she murmured, encouraging him to come closer.

Her fingers trembled as Jericho's hovered close. Then, in one quick movement, she made a fist and slashed upward. The amethyst cut a sharp line over Jericho's cheek and brow, and he stumbled back with a yell.

Now, run! she screamed at herself.

But Jericho whipped around and backhanded her across the face with enough force to rattle her teeth. She landed with a grunt, blinking with double vision.

"Bitch. I'll teach you."

Jericho lifted her like a puppet and tossed her down again. She landed on her back with the wind knocked out of her, and her whole world lurched and went sideways. Even Jericho seemed to pause for a moment and look around.

Dawn placed her palms again the ground. Wait — had she imagined the ground shaking under her, or had that really happened?

A ferocious growl split the night, and Dawn screamed at the sight of an oncoming bear. A silent scream that finished with her mouth wide open as the bear rushed at Jericho.

"Hunter?" she whispered, wobbling to her feet.

The bear's roar thundered through her ears, and she crumpled, still dizzy. Her hand bashed the ground, and the earth rumbled. A real rumble, not something she imagined.

"You," Jericho grunted as the bear jumped at him.

"Hunter!" she cried.

Her vision filled with spots as she scanned the slope behind him. Were the other shifters approaching, or had Hunter overcome them all?

She stared, but no other living creature took shape on the slope. It was just her, Hunter, and Jericho now.

Hunter pushed Jericho toward the cliff, but his foe simply shoved back with power that belied his size. Hunter attacked a second time, but Jericho forced him away with a swipe of his knife.

"Try me, little cub. Try me."

His voice was so mocking, so cruel, that Dawn thumped her fist on the ground. That time, the whole cliff shook, and even Jericho paused before goading Hunter on. "Come and get me, cub."

Dawn clutched the ground, still confused. Had that been a minor earthquake?

The amethyst shone in the moonlight, and she held it up, forcing her rattled mind to think things through.

Earthquake... Earthstone...

Hunter and Jericho battled on, but she tuned them out. When Regina had stomped on the ground, the whole cliff felt as if it might give way. Regina had done quite a lot of shoving over the past few days, and Dawn had been surprised at the slender woman's power.

She held up the Spirit Stone, and it finally clicked. The Earthstone had been lending some of its power to Regina. The Earthstone had made the cliff shake.

I can do it again. The amethyst seemed to wink.

Jericho coaxed Hunter forward, and Dawn wondered if she dared test her crazy hypothesis.

Hunter was limping, his fur stained crimson. Jericho, on the other hand, was relatively fresh. Her eyes narrowed on him, and she gave in to the anger welling up inside. That man had killed Hunter's mother and who knew how many others. A man who felt entitled to kill and rape on whim.

She formed a fist and held it high above the ground. Watching. Waiting.

Hunter rushed Jericho again, and her heart wailed for him. Such courage. Such devotion. Such perseverance regardless of the odds.

She bared her teeth like a wild animal and forced herself to watch. Jericho swung the knife, but Hunter ducked just in time. He rammed into Jericho and pushed him toward the cliff's edge. But Jericho bent an elbow and smashed it into Hunter's soft black nose.

A bone cracked. The bear roared in frustration. Jericho jeered.

Dawn trembled, waiting for her chance. Would it come too late?

The grizzly reared on his back legs, but Jericho kicked him in the ribs, sending Hunter tumbling downslope.

There. Now!

Heat surged from the ring and spread throughout Dawn's body, sending as clear a signal as she could wish for. She thumped her fist against the ground. Once. Twice.

The earth rumbled, and Jericho threw his arms out for balance. His head snapped her way, and his eyes narrowed.

She struck the ground again, ignoring the pain of the impact.

This man must die, she told the Earthstone. She — the woman who'd always believed in law and order and the power

153

of the judiciary — was suddenly issuing death warrants. There was no other way.

Help me, she whispered, smashing her fist into the ground once more.

The cliff rumbled, making Jericho lurch and sway.

"Stop that," he yelled, shuffling closer like a drunk.

Help me rid the world of this evil, she cried, beating on the earth.

A roar built all around her. At first, she thought it as Hunter, coming back for another try. But it was the ground, not Hunter, and the rumbling increased.

"I said—" Jericho demanded. Then his eyes went wide.

She held his gaze steadily and showed him her fist. The amethyst glittered in the darkness before she brought her hand down one more time — and kept it there.

Vibrations rippled through the earth, up her arm, and through her body, immobilizing her. She was on her hands and knees, facing upslope, watching the earth shake. Jericho flailed for balance as a fissure opened between them, zigzagging across the outcrop.

"No!" Jericho screamed.

"Yes," she whispered.

The earth thundered. Rocks tumbled. Jericho screamed. Dawn crawled backward as the slope before her tilted and crumbled into the sea. Jericho's arms grabbed at thin air, and then he, too, plummeted as the top of the cliff collapsed.

Dawn stared at the rockslide, frozen at the very lip of the drop-off. A mess of boulders and dirt disappeared into the crashing surf along with the body of her foe.

Her heart hammered as she lifted her hand off the ground — gently, as if releasing a grenade. The earth ceased shaking, and the sound of surf replaced that of the rockslide. She backed up slowly, staring. Then she rushed to the bear that lay bleeding on the grass.

"Hunter..."

She fell to her knees, hugging him. Not caring that it was coarse fur under her hand instead of smooth skin, because either way, the soul inside that body was Hunter's.

"Hunter, please. . ." she begged, watching for some sign of life. Then she cried out, because the earth seemed to be moving again. "No," she croaked.

She looked around wildly, but it wasn't the earth. It was only her, rising and falling in a regular pattern. Hunter was breathing, moving his chest up and down, and moving her with it.

"Hunter! Are you okay?"

The bear raised its head, wincing. Slowly, it batted its long eyelashes.

She cupped his muzzle. "Please, tell me you're okay."

The bear chuffed faintly then dropped its head again. She sat beside him, petting the one patch of his thick fur unstained by blood. Her hand throbbed, but she paid it no heed. What were a few broken bones? As long as no other evil shifter turned up, she and Hunter were okay.

"Dawn," he murmured, and her eyes flew open in surprise.

Whoa. He'd been quietly shifting under her very touch. She was so shaken, she'd barely noticed.

"Dawn," he said, pulling her to his side.

She curled her body around him in a huge hug. He'd done enough fighting and protecting. It was her turn to take care of him.

"You're amazing," he whispered in a creaky voice.

She brushed a hand along his cheek. "You're the amazing one."

An owl hooted from the woods at the base of the hill, and for a moment, the earth felt at peace. Even when a tiger padded out of the shadows and chuffed, Dawn remained calm.

"Cruz," Hunter murmured. "Man, do I owe you."

The tiger blinked his yellow-green eyes. *Yes, you do,* he seemed to say.

"Where is he going?" Dawn asked when Cruz turned with a swish of his tail. "Is he okay?" A gash drew a jagged line down his side, and he walked with a limp.

"He's going back to the beach to clean up. And, yeah, he'll be okay."

155

Clean up meant dispose of the bodies, Dawn figured, but at that point, she didn't care. At least, not until a moment later, when a huge shadow whooshed overhead.

"Whoa." She ducked.

Hunter just nodded and waved. "That's Kai."

Dawn gaped.

Sure. You can see dragons here from time to time, Lily had once said.

Dawn worked her jaw loose again. She and Lily were going to have to have a long talk one of these days.

"What other shifters are you friends with—"

She stopped and gaped. Whoa. Hunter was naked. Very naked. But she barely had time to process that thought when voices broke out not too far away. She looked downhill, alarmed. Now what?

"Oh, brother," Hunter murmured.

A group of people was rushing out from the resort — party-goers and resort staff, roused by the rockslide. Some gestured, while others ran forward to inspect the damage.

Hunter's hand wrapped around hers, hiding the glowing ring.

"What happened?" a man shouted.

Dawn hid her face against Hunter's chest. How were they going to explain a shifter fight, Spirit Stones, and being naked at the edge of a fresh rockslide?

"The whole cliff fell," someone replied.

The footsteps grew louder, closer.

"I knew this slope was unstable," another person said.

"The surf probably undercut the whole thing."

Dawn shook her head against Hunter's chest. *Nope. Try again.*

"Wait a minute, what are you doing here?" a woman cried, staring at them.

Hunter's face was an inch from Dawn's, and she looked right into his eyes, whispering. "What are we going to say?"

His cracked lips curled into a grin. "You trust me?"

Dawn nodded and whispered back. "Yes. You never have to ask me that again, by the way."

His grin grew wider, and he pressed his lips against hers. His hands tightened around her back, and he rolled slightly, covering her.

It was the craziest possible time for a kiss, but she was all in. Her mouth opened under his, her lips nibbling gently. Her heart beat faster.

"Hey, what are you two doing up here?" a fresh arrival demanded.

"Holy crap. The cliff fell away, and you're making out?" someone else said.

Dawn suppressed a giggle but went right on kissing Hunter. She could imagine the jokes she'd have to endure at headquarters when the guys heard about her being found half naked and wrapped around a security guard while on the clock.

Must have been some sex, she figured the first wisecrack would go.

Did he make your world shake, Dawn? would probably come next.

And they'd go on and on, and the whole thing would get out of control.

Dawn grinned under her kiss and snuggled closer. Somehow, she didn't care about any of that. And in a way, it was true. Hunter had shaken her world. In the best possible way.

Chapter Sixteen

Three days later. . .

"Mmm," Hunter murmured, rolling in his bed.

A sea breeze whispered over the lawn outside, and a honeycreeper chirped from the trees. The curtains stirred lazily, and though he couldn't see it, he could imagine the morning sunlight sparkling off a calm sea.

Hunter stretched slowly under the sheets, relishing the warm, limber feeling of his limbs. Nothing beat waking up slowly, prolonging the transition from dreamtime to real life.

Real life is even better than a dream, his bear said with a smug yawn.

He flexed his fingers over Dawn's and snuggled her closer. Everything was okay. More than okay — everything was perfect. The Vanderpelt wedding was over. The Rolls Royce was back in the garage, and best of all, Dawn was in his bed, tucked close to him.

His bear was right. Sometimes, real life was better than a dream — though both were pretty damn good. He'd been dreaming of an idyllic Maui wedding. Not Regina's — God, no. That had fallen apart the night the little brat threw her engagement ring into the sea. The newspapers, of course, had been all over the story in the following days.

Celebrity bride jilts groom, cancels wedding of the century.

Divers on the hunt for missing $100,000 ring.

Teary bride seen leaving Maui on private jet. Flower bill unpaid.

All of Maui exhaled when the Vanderpelts departed, it seemed.

ANNA LOWE

The papers were so busy with gossip that the disappearance of Jericho Deroux was a mere footnote on page three of the *Maui News. Alaskan Pipeline Boss Missing — Lost in Surf?*

Hunter tightened his arms around Dawn. When he kissed her shoulder, she sighed and turned in his arms, giving him a sleepy smile. "Good morning."

Best morning of my life, his bear murmured for the third day in a row. Hunter figured he'd be saying that every morning for the rest of his life.

"Morning," he whispered, gently brushing a finger over her cheek.

Her eyes fluttered closed, and her chest rose in deep, sleepy breaths.

"Is that you purring?" she mumbled a second later.

"That's Keiki."

The calico kitten had disappeared early the previous night, as she always did when the bedroom heated up. Which meant Keiki had spent most of the previous seventy-two hours elsewhere — most likely with Cruz, considering how much time Hunter and Dawn had spent wrapped around each other in sweaty ecstasy. For now, Keiki was back, settled comfortably on the mattress behind Dawn, purring more loudly than such a tiny thing ought to be capable of.

"Mmm. I had the best dream," Dawn murmured.

Hunter twirled a wisp of her silky hair — another dream come true — as he waited for more.

"A wedding. Our wedding."

His breath caught in his throat. He'd been dreaming the same thing.

"You and me and a handful of guests, right here on the lawn at Koa Point," Dawn went on.

Hunter's hand trembled a little in the kitten's soft fur. He'd imagined it the exact same way. Just him and Dawn with the handful of guests. The people who really mattered. Kai, Cruz, Boone, and Silas — the men he'd been through so much with over the years — and of course Tessa, Nina, Lily, Dawn's mother, and a few of Dawn's friends.

160

"Was Lily wearing a pink and orange muumuu?" he asked, holding perfectly still.

Dawn's eyes shot open. "How did you know?"

"I had the same dream."

The other details matched too, as they discovered in talking it over.

"There was a beautiful vase of wild iris and another of pitaya," Dawn murmured.

Hunter swallowed the lump in his throat before answering. "The iris is for my mother and the pitaya for Georgia Mae, my foster mother."

Dawn ran a hand down his arm, and the sorrow eased away again.

"Georgia Mae," Dawn murmured. "I was wondering about her. You said she was an owl shifter, right?"

He nodded her along silently.

"Do you think that has anything to do with me and my *aumakua*?"

He smoothed a hand over Dawn's silky hair and looked deep into her eyes. "Honestly? I don't know. It could be that her spirit and your *aumakua* connect somehow. All I know is that destiny has its own way of revealing things."

They stared at each other, letting the seconds tick by as they chewed the thought over. But destiny was such a mystery to Hunter, he never got far thinking it through. He was just grateful to have been granted his mate.

Maybe the wedding wasn't a dream, his bear whispered, full of hope. *Maybe it was a vision.*

Hunter's lips moved, but he didn't say anything. He couldn't say anything. He just hoped and hoped, losing himself in the depths of Dawn's dark eyes.

"I like the idea of a wedding," he ventured at last. Most shifters didn't bother, but never mind that — he'd be happy for any and all forms of making a vow to his mate.

"I like the idea, too," she said.

His chest tightened as if his heart had just swelled to twice its size.

"Really?"

161

She nodded. "Really."

He played back over his dream until he got to the "I do" part.

"Really?" he whispered, just to make sure.

She laughed then kissed him. "Really."

He closed his eyes, trying not to get too far ahead of himself with visions of all the happy years ahead. He and Dawn could spend some time settling in together. Maybe a couple of years down the line, if Dawn agreed, they could have a few cubs. Cubs that would be cherished, loved, and above all, protected by the shifters of Koa Point. Maybe he could take them and Dawn to see Alaska someday. Maybe. . .

He reeled his thoughts back in before he got all the way up to growing old with Dawn — but hell, that sounded like bliss, too.

"You know what else I dreamed about?" Dawn added. Her voice grew lower, edgier.

He stroked her shoulders. "What?"

She ran a hand over his bare chest and up to her neck. "The mating bite," she whispered.

His heart beat faster. Harder. She'd said *dream* not *nightmare*, right?

He'd done his best to explain everything to her over the past few days, vowing never to keep a secret from his true love again. The whole time, he'd been terrified that the details would freak her out. After all, having three-inch fangs puncture your throat would sound pretty barbaric to a human, though mated shifters called the experience the high of their lives.

"Nina said—"

Hunter's head popped off the pillow. "Nina?"

Dawn blushed. "She, Tessa, and I had a girls' talk yesterday. Remember, while you guys did the dishes and we walked down to the beach?"

Hunter blanched, wondering how much graphic detail they had shared. He studied Dawn's face, blushing a little. She was blushing too. But when he looked closer, he realized the pink hue didn't stem from fear or embarrassment. It was arousal.

He sniffed covertly and, yes — there it was. The sweet, sugary scent in the air.

Dawn fluttered her eyelids shyly before going on. "Nina said it was amazing. Tessa did, too."

Hunter made a mental note to hunt down the nicest flowers on Maui for those two.

His bear grinned inside, and a slow, languid heat wave spread through his veins.

Dawn's hand trailed up and down his chest, dipping lower every time, making his cock hard. Her eyes shone brighter. Her fingers pressed more firmly on his skin until his cock strained upward, desperate for her touch.

He shifted his hands from her waist to her sides, teasing her breasts.

"Nina said she liked it so much, they do it all the time."

Hunter wasn't sure he wanted to hear much more about Nina and Boone's sex life, but yes, he'd heard about that, too. That the mating bite could be repeated as a couple renewed their bond throughout their lives.

Dawn drew her ankle along his calf. Her hair fanned out over the pillow, and her nipples peaked. When he eased his hand over her breast, she arched her back and groaned.

"Hunter, I don't just want the mating bite. I need it," she said in an achy, urgent voice. She drew her leg higher along his, opening to him. On the next downstroke of her hand, she teased her fingers over his cock.

Hunter sucked in a breath. He'd fought off the urge to claim his mate for so long, he thought he'd go crazy. The quiet bliss of the past few days had taken the edge off, but the moment Dawn mentioned mating, the burning need came back.

He rolled over her and pinned her free hand over her head, leaving just enough space between their bodies for her to keep one hand wrapped around his cock.

"Sorry, Keiki," Dawn giggled as the kitten fled.

"Bye, Keiki," he murmured then turned to Dawn, growing serious. "Mating is forever. More permanent and more complete than marriage can ever be."

"Good." Her eyes blazed.

"It's not just for a lifetime. They say the bond holds into the afterlife."

"I want that, Hunter. I want you."

He closed his eyes, feeling as if he could skip through a field of wildflowers. As if there were a dozen harps playing in the room next door hitting a high, yearning note.

His hands trembled, a lot like his voice. "I want you, Dawn. I wanted you for years. More than anything. But you need to be sure. It will make you a shifter, too."

She reared off the mattress to press her lips to his. "Does this feel sure?"

The second her mouth covered his, he moaned.

"Does this feel sure?" she murmured, running her hand up and down his cock.

Fireworks exploded throughout his body, setting off jolts of desire. His cock pushed at her hip as he lowered his head to her breast, unable to hold back.

"Yes..." she panted, arching into him. "Yes..."

He'd only meant to brush his lips over her nipple, but he ended up consuming it, rolling the tight bud between his lips and sucking hard.

"Yes..." she groaned. "Hunter..."

She released his cock, grabbed his free hand, and guided it between her legs. "Please, Hunter."

Over the past few days, they'd bounced between sheer ecstasy and limp bliss dozens of times, but the urgency that gripped them now was something entirely new. As if a flame ignited by destiny at the end of a long fuse had finally reached the dynamite.

Now, his body screamed. *Claim her now.*

He circled his hand over her core, then dipped inside. One finger then two, moving easily, spreading her slick heat.

She's ready. So, so ready, his bear cried, feeling her flesh yield under his.

Dawn gripped his shoulders and cried his name.

He stretched his hand wide, circling her clit with his thumb while his fingers probed deeper.

"So good," she moaned, lifting her hips toward his.

He released her breast, took a quick breath, and claimed her mouth again. Insistently. Moving his tongue over hers the way he wanted to let his cock stroke over her sex.

Dawn — his beautiful, controlled Dawn — writhed and mumbled under his body, letting it all go.

She likes letting go, his bear said. *She needs to let go.*

He plunged his fingers and tongue deeper, faster, driving her body further and further into a sensual cloud. Dawn pushed desperately against him, scraping her nails over his back.

Hunter...

He swore he could hear her hungry cries in his mind.

I can. I do, his bear hummed.

In a dizzying rush, he put his hands beside her head, nudged her legs wider, and centered his cock over her entrance, where it pulsed greedily.

What are you waiting for? his bear cried.

Dawn's eyes flew open and locked on his.

That. That was what he was waiting for. That extra connection. That assurance that she was absolutely, positively sure.

The second she nodded, he plunged in.

The high hit him in six places at once. His cock burned, relishing the tight squeeze. His head tilted back, and his lips threw silent groans at the ceiling. His hips thrust, almost pushing him off-balance.

"Yes..." Dawn moaned, moving in time with him.

It wasn't him making love to her so much as fate orchestrating a masterpiece, and all he could do was ride the wave that swept both of them away.

He dropped to his elbows, huffing into her neck as their rhythm quickened. Dawn's hair formed a curtain, trapping her incredible scent. He pressed his face closer to her skin, pumping his hips the whole time.

Neck... Mate... Mine... his bear chanted inside.

When he nipped the soft skin of her neck, Dawn tipped her head, making space for him. He flicked his tongue, tasting her, searching for the spot, letting instinct guide him. Running his

ANNA LOWE

stubbly chin up and down the notch of her neck, he could sense
her pulse, feel the waves of heat course under her skin.

"Hunter..." she moaned, clutching the back of his head.

His canines extended in a slow, painful slide that felt almost
as good as Dawn clenching over his cock.

Mate... his bear called. *Mine...*

He scraped his teeth over her skin until the pressure building in his body grew too much to bear.

At the exact moment that he exploded inside her, he bit.

Hunter sank his teeth deep and hung on. The sensation
was like being caught in the waves that had carried them to
shore a few days earlier, but in a good way. That rush of sound
and sensation. That sense of some greater force taking control.
The instinct to hold his breath and clench every muscle tight.

Dawn clutched at him the way she had on the beach, and
her body shuddered again and again.

So good... Yes... More... she begged.

He could hear her thoughts. Could she hear his?

My mate... Love you... Need you...

Slowly, he withdrew his teeth but kept his lips sealed around
her neck as his shifter essence circulated through her veins.

Time to let go, instinct murmured a few heartbeats later.

But he never wanted to let go.

You are bonded now. It's time to let go.

He tightened his arms around Dawn's body, letting his lips
soften gradually. He ran his tongue over the bite mark, feeling
the skin heal as he released.

She is safe. You can let go.

He dropped free and panted into the pillow beside her head,
progressively releasing every taut muscle in his body.

"Oh my God," Dawn whispered.

He froze. Was she hurt? Bleeding? Full of regret?

She hummed, going boneless against him. "That feels so
good."

Hunter let out a long, relieved breath.

"Promise me we get to do that again...and again?" she
breathed.

Hunter laughed — a laugh that started deep in his heart and rumbled through his chest before eventually escaping to the room. "I promise," he said, hugging her tight. "I promise, my mate."

Epilogue

"So, what happens now?" Cruz growled.

Dawn pursed her lips, looking at the men and women gathered in the meeting house at Koa Point that evening. A sea breeze drifted in and out of the open structure much like little Keiki wound around Dawn's legs. Crickets chirped all around, and tiny sparks snapped upward from the tiki torches that lit the paths converging on the meeting house.

Hours earlier, Dawn had experienced the high of her life. She'd been glowing from the mating bite all afternoon. Then she'd slept the soundest sleep of her life, and her body still tingled. In fact, she'd been sleeping well ever since coming to Koa Point. Which probably had more to do with the reassuring grip of Hunter's arms around her than the modest comforts of the cottage he lived in. The house was a pretty, green structure with white trim, built in classic plantation style. A place that felt so much like home, she would have been happy to move right in. She even had a corner picked out for her antique Victrola. They had agreed to a week at her place and a week at his, for starters, but she could already tell where they'd end up. And, heck, who could blame her? Koa Point Estate was amazing, and the gates seemed to hold the troubles of the world at bay.

At some point in the blissful haze of the afternoon, Boone had come along to call them to the meeting, and anxiety tinged the edges of her world again.

"What are you doing?" she'd asked when Hunter rubbed his shoulder against the doorframe on the way out of the cottage.

His eyes dropped in chagrin. "It's kind of a bear thing," he shrugged, trying to downplay what she sensed was significant. "We like to mark our turf."

She'd laughed, but when he kept his shoulder pressed against hers in the meeting house, a happy little shiver went through her. A shiver that said, *I'm his, and he's mine.*

And boy did she need him now. Night had fallen, the meeting had begun, and Cruz's grim words silenced the room.

So, what happens now?

Dawn forced herself not to fidget as she looked around.

The shifters of Koa Point were all there — in human form, thank goodness. Although she'd learned her lesson about good and bad shifters, a little bit of anxiety remained when she faced the others. Boone and Nina, who could both shift into wolf form. Cruz, the tiger she owed her life to. Kai, Tessa, and Silas, who were all dragon shifters. Dragons, for goodness' sake!

You'll be a shifter soon, too, Hunter had explained to her.

Strangely, the thought didn't terrify her. In fact, she was curious what it would be like. Still, living among so many shifters would take a lot of getting used to.

Having Hunter there helped, as did Keiki. The kitten skipped over to Cruz's legs and purred loudly. When Cruz — lean, hard-faced Cruz, who carried the same kind of wounded warrior vibe Hunter once had — smiled slightly and scooped the kitten up against his chest, Dawn's jaw nearly dropped. He held Keiki protectively, staring into the distance, stroking her fur. The man was more like Hunter than she'd guessed. A protector, not an instigator. A man who would lay down his life for a noble cause.

But Hunter had shed that sad veneer he'd always carried with him. He practically glowed, as did she. Cruz, on the other hand...

"Good question," Kai said. "What happens now?"

All eyes swung to Silas, the leader of the Koa Point shifters. He scraped a hand through his dark hair and looked at Dawn.

What? What did he want?

170

Hunter cleared his throat and nudged her, and she remembered. The amethyst. The Spirit Stone. She drew the ring slowly out of her pocket and laid it on the table.

"The Earthstone," Silas murmured.

Everyone leaned closer. Then Tessa pulled a necklace over her head and placed it on the table beside the ring. Dawn's mouth cracked open at the sight of the emerald strung on the silver chain.

"The Lifestone," Hunter said in a hushed voice.

"Look," Tessa whispered as both gems started to glow.

Silas nodded wearily and signaled to Nina, who placed a huge ruby beside the other gems. The Firestone started to glow, until all three were blazing like embers in a freshly stoked fire.

"The Firestone."

Dawn stared at the trio of precious stones. If only Lily were here — she'd have a comment to break the tension in the room, for sure. But Dawn could only stand and gape.

They have special powers, Hunter had said. *Powers most humans aren't aware of.*

She swallowed the lump in her throat, remembering the jolt of energy the amethyst had sent through her body when she'd first slipped the ring on her finger.

"Do they each control an element?" she ventured.

Silas shook his head. "The names are more symbolic than literal, from what I can tell. The Earthstone represents all facets of nature, I believe. But so much of dragon lore has been lost..." He trailed off, shaking his head.

Kai motioned toward the amethyst. "It was in front of our eyes the whole time. Regina was wearing this ring. Why couldn't we sense it earlier?"

Everyone looked at Silas, but he raised an eyebrow at Hunter and waited for the bear shifter to speak.

Hunter's fingers tightened around hers, and she squeezed back.

"I think the amethyst was slumbering," Hunter said. "It was only when the diamond was brought close that the amethyst was stirred to life."

171

"Why the diamond? It's not a Spirit Stone," Nina asked.

"Gems are like jealous women," Boone said. When Nina smacked his arm, he jabbed a finger in Silas's direction. "His words, honey. Not mine."

"Silas — seriously?" Tessa put her hands on her hips.

Dawn hid her grin. She liked these women. The room practically pulsed with alpha hormones, but Tessa and Nina weren't intimidated in the least. In some ways, it was similar to the male-dominated police squad. These shifters were on a whole different level than Dawn's colleagues, but still. She relaxed slightly. Yes, she could handle it here.

Hunter looked at her, all muscle and soft eyes, and she grinned. Yep. She could definitely handle it here.

Silas shrugged. "Dragon lore. You know how it is."

Tessa made a face and muttered something like, "Still learning."

"In any case," Silas continued, "That seems to have been the catalyst."

"But Regina didn't make the cliff collapse," Kai pointed out.

"I think Dawn being in touch with her *aumakua* must have helped direct and amplify its power," Silas said, giving her a respectful nod.

She rolled her lips over each other, grateful for the ancestral spirits that swooped in to guide her at the most critical times.

Boone clapped his hands in a that's-that gesture. "Well, the Earthstone is ours now."

Hunter glared. "It's Dawn's."

"Whoa. No. Wait," she said quickly.

"You fished it out of the ocean." Kai pointed out.

"Possibly, but as a member of the Maui Police Department... Let's just say I'd rather not bend another rule. God knows I've done enough of that lately."

Hunter looked downcast at the remark, so she squeezed his hand. "I took a vow, right? But I understand that some things have to operate outside the law — as long as we stay within the spirit of the law. Besides, it seems to me the human world is better off without something this powerful in its hands."

Silas rubbed his jaw thoughtfully. "Sometimes I think the shifter world would be better off without it, too."

"What would Jericho have done with the Earthstone?" Dawn asked and regretted it when Hunter's shoulder went hard.

"I did some digging around," Kai said. "Apparently, he's been trying to push through this oil pipeline for years. The proposed route would slice through pristine wilderness — some of it shifter territory—"

Dawn hugged Hunter's arm, thinking of what he'd been through as a cub.

"—so I'd say Jericho would have used to it overpower the last holdouts."

"You did it, man." Boone grinned at Hunter. "You stopped him."

Hunter shook his head. "Dawn stopped him."

"The Earthstone stopped him," she corrected. "But it's here now. That's good, right?" she asked in the heavy silence that ensued. "You can keep it safe."

Silas nodded slowly. Wearily. "We'll do our best. But the Spirit Stones call to one another. Which means the other two..."

Every face in the room fell, and Cruz held Keiki a little tighter.

Hunter caught Dawn's perplexed look and filled in the rest. "The other two could turn up anytime."

"And considering what we went through to secure these..." Kai added, pulling Tessa closer.

Seconds ticked by in weighty silence.

"Hey, the Spirit Stones brought us blessings, too. Right?" Boone said, sliding his arm over Nina's shoulders.

Dawn looked around the room. Kai and Tessa had found each other through the emerald. Boone and Nina met because of the ruby. And, as for herself... Dawn gripped Hunter's hand tighter. The amethyst had brought her the man she'd secretly loved for years.

She looked at Cruz and Silas, the only two bachelors left in the gang. Would destiny bring them true love, too?

"So, what do we do?" she asked, eyeing the jewels.

Silas's gaze traveled from face to face, and then he shook his head. "We watch. We wait."

* THE END *

Sneak Peek: Lure of the Tiger

Tiger shifter Cruz Khala doesn't trust humans, and for good reason. He doesn't trust destiny, either — not even when it sends him the one woman capable of waking the sunny side of his tortured soul. But there's more than love at stake as merciless shifter forces converge on sunny Maui, all of them intent on stealing a priceless jewel with mysterious powers.

Sneak Peek: Lure of the Tiger
Chapter 1

Cruz steadied his breath and squinted across the moonlit land-scape. The sea breeze teased his hair as he crouched, scanning for his target. The barrel of the rifle felt cool in his hands, much like the wind cooled the sweat on his back. The palm trees that concealed him whispered an urgent warning as he focused intently on the crowd gathered at the golf club half a mile away.

Something didn't feel right, but he fought the feeling away. When did a hit ever feel right?

The voice of his informant echoed through his mind for the thousandth time. *Northwest corner of the terrace. Look for a guest in black with black-rimmed glasses. The waiter will hand that guest a cocktail glass marked with a pink umbrella and an olive with a green toothpick. That guest is your target.*

Easy, he tried convincing himself.

But, hell. He must have lost his touch, because doubts crowded his mind. Not too long ago, in his active duty days, he'd been the top sniper in his elite Special Forces unit, and he'd never hesitated when it came to getting a job done. But that was war. This was...

This is war, too, his inner tiger insisted. *Finally, we get revenge on the monster who murdered our family.*

Cruz forced away the lump in his throat and blinked hard. *Get your shit together, soldier.*

Technically, he wasn't a soldier any more, but that was just on paper. The soldier part would always be in his blood, just as his tiger side was part of his blood. He was made to fight. To protect. To battle for just causes in a deeply troubled world.

And revenge was as just a cause as any, especially when he considered the cruel manner in which his entire family had been wiped out. His parents. His younger sister. His brother. All of them killed in cold blood.

A movement stirred on the side terrace, away from the crowd, and he refocused through the sights. A woman in a sequin dress danced out of the French doors, giggling, followed by a man who only had eyes for her ass.

Cruz rolled his eyes. Definitely not his target.

A moment later, two businessmen stepped out onto the terrace, and the amorous couple scurried into the shadows of the garden. The newcomers didn't walk to the northwest corner of the terrace, but they stopped close enough to make Cruz's shoulders tense with anticipation. When a waiter appeared, Cruz held his breath, steadying his pulse the way he would if ready to pounce on his prey.

He adjusted the sights to get a better look at the drinks on the waiter's tray. Straight up bourbon, from the look of it. No miniature umbrellas. No toothpicks or olives.

He exhaled. Not his target. Still, he watched the men. Something about their tailored suits and self-important stances made him suspicious. But then again, what did he expect from a couple of humans? Humans were unpredictable. Irrational. Dangerous.

A cloud slid over the moon. No problem – there was plenty of light on that terrace. But when another shadow moved in the doorway, his blood rushed and heated. His nose twitched, and every nerve in his body jolted with shocks of warning. His brow furrowed, suddenly on high alert.

Alert against what? His heart thumped.

Never in his life had he felt this strong a premonition. Not the day his family had been murdered, nor the split second before his convoy had been trapped in an ambush, three years ago. Not even the day he'd met Silas, Kai, Boone, and Hunter, the shifters who were to become his brothers in arms. Destiny had forewarned him of each of those events, if only in a frustratingly vague way and only seconds before the shit hit the fan.

This felt exactly the same. His shoulders squared. Something big was about to happen and change his life forever.

Cruz forced himself to breathe evenly. That feeling was to be expected the day he finally had the chance to avenge his family, right?

The curtains at the doors to the terrace stirred, and the two men turned to see who it was. Cruz pressed his finger against the trigger, ready to fire while his inner tiger twitched its tail.

"Come on, already," he whispered when the person at the doorway hesitated. His lips brushed against the barrel, and the acrid taste of metal filled his mouth.

Focus, damn it. Focus.

He turned his sights on the figure in the doorway. Was that his target?

One of the men made a motion, and a woman stepped into view. Proud. Graceful. But... sad, too. Conflicted, somehow.

The gears of his mind ticked over in agonizingly slow motion, and none of the messages firing through his nerves made sense. Why was she sad? And why did that seem so heart-wrenchingly important to him?

The thick-rimmed glasses propped back on her head didn't match her fair, wavy hair, just like her glum expression didn't fit her cheerily freckled face.

Another man pushed outside, passing the woman close enough to make her long, black dress swish. Cruz swung the rifle toward him — a big guy whose combed-back hair didn't hide the bare patches on his scalp. The fancy suit didn't quite hide the fact that the man's gut hung over his belt, either.

The two businessmen nodded and disappeared inside, leaving the big man talking to the woman. More like talking at her while her shoulders lifted in a hidden sigh. She turned her face up to the sky and closed her eyes. When the man stepped closer — too close — the woman flinched and stepped away.

"Slimeball," Cruz murmured.

Slimeball, his tiger agreed. The type it would be so, so easy to kill. Arrogant, manipulative, and self-assured. Cruz could see all that in the man's viper eyes.

Cruz pursed his lips. Was that his target?

Every instinct in his body tugged his attention to the woman, making it hard to focus on the man she obviously deplored. When Slimeball slithered closer to her lithe body, her whole body tensed, and she rubbed her hands over her crossed arms. Was that hate glittering in her eyes?

Cruz was so mesmerized, he barely paid attention when someone else joined the woman and the big man. Then a white sleeve rose at the woman's side... a waiter, offering her a drink.

Cruz's heart stopped.

Guest in black with black-rimmed glasses. The waiter will hand that guest a cocktail glass with a pink umbrella and a green toothpick. That's your target.

Cruz flicked his eyes to the drink. Pink umbrella. Green toothpick.

Holy shit. The woman was his target? That woman was responsible for the deaths of the people he loved?

The clouds slipped clear of the moon as commands thundered through his mind.

Shoot her!

Spare her!

Pull the trigger!

Don't! Don't!

He clenched his jaw. Maybe something had gone wrong. Maybe his informant was wrong — terribly wrong. But damn it, how was that possible? How?

If it had been Slimeball holding that cocktail, Cruz would have squeezed off a round and slipped away into the night without a second thought. But the woman...

The joints of his fingers seized up, refusing to pull the trigger.

She could be the killer. Humans are tricky that way, his tiger said, but even he didn't sound convinced.

180

Cruz considered. Even if she wasn't the killer, what did he care? Humans were responsible for most of the problems of the world. What harm would one less human do?

Then he caught himself. God, was he jaded. Was he really willing to kill a woman who could be innocent?

He studied her head to toe. The truth was, she didn't look like a killer. She didn't have the stance of a killer. Cruz knew; he'd crossed paths with enough in his day to be able to tell. Men and women both, and this woman didn't fit in. He sniffed the air. She didn't smell like a killer, either.

On the contrary, she smelled nice. His tiger purred, teasing her scent out of all those tangled in the sweet night air. *Like a sea breeze. Like wild roses that grow in the edge of the beach.*

Cruz frowned. Usually, he could settle his racing pulse down with sheer mind control. But now, his heart revved just from looking at her. What the hell was wrong with him?

Destiny, a voice growled in the recesses of his mind.

He shivered in spite of himself. Destiny, what?

But that was it. One cryptic whisper from who knows what dark corner of the universe, and nothing more.

"Destiny." He cursed under his breath.

Some shifters revered a benign form of destiny that they swore brought goodness and hope and love. Others knew the truth, as Cruz did: that destiny was a fickle, manipulative, and mysterious power that was just as likely to fuck up a man's life as show him the path to bliss. Destiny didn't pay attention to mere mortals often, but when it did, it was best to stay the hell away and hole up far away from its interference. Someplace like his cabin, tucked deep in the woods at Koa Point, where no one could bother him. Not even Fate.

Still, he moved his finger off the trigger and watched the woman closely. She made a chopping motion said something that made Slimeball shake a finger at her. Then she turned away with a firm set to her shoulders, prompting Slimeball to stalk back into the building, leaving her alone.

Cruz's finger jumped back to the trigger. This was his chance, right? The silenced rifle wouldn't make much noise, and no one would notice her body thump to the ground. That would give Cruz more time to cover his tracks. He could finish this mission, head home, and maybe even find a little peace in knowing he'd avenged his family at last.

Don't shoot her. Don't! His tiger growled. *She's not the killer.*

Wait a second. His tiger was usually the one desperate for revenge. Now the beast wanted to spare the woman? How did he know she was innocent?

Killers don't look at the stars like they're looking for answers, his tiger said.

Cruz watched as the woman raised her glass and whispered a toast to the stars.

Not a toast. A promise, his tiger insisted. *And killers don't shift from foot to foot like they wish they were somewhere else. They focus.*

That, Cruz had to agree with. If a person could teleport from one place to another, he'd bet that woman would be out of that pretentious club in a flash. Out of that silk dress, too. She looked more like the cutoff jeans and flip-flop type.

His tiger grinned. *I like her.*

Which was nuts. He didn't like humans. Especially one who might be his mortal enemy.

She's not our mortal enemy. She's our m—

Cruz cut the thought off and jerked his head right, staring east, where something caught his attention. Not so much a motion as the sense that someone was there. After a moment of searching, his keen feline eyes caught sight of a man. One second, the figure was there, and the next, he was hidden by the foliage. Then he was visible again and, holy shit — screwing together two long, metal shafts. An M110 — a sniper's rifle much like Cruz's.

His first reaction was outrage. That woman on the terrace was his target — nobody else's. No one was going to have the satisfaction of eliminating that murderer but him.

In a flash, he swung his rifle back to the woman on the terrace and took aim.

Satisfaction? She's not a killer, a little voice insisted.

The woman gazed up at the stars, and the electric current that zapped through Cruz's body just wouldn't let up. He bared his teeth, ready to shoot that voice instead of a target half a mile away. But, hell. What if the woman was innocent? What if he never found out?

The woman turned, ready to head inside. Meaning it was now or never if he was going to get a shot off before the other sniper did.

Now, the dark side of his soul called.

Never! his tiger growled.

He glanced to the right, where the second man was hurriedly taking aim at the woman.

No, his tiger roared. *No!*

A pop sounded, followed by an outbreak of laughter from the crowd on the main porch.

What the hell? Cruz's heart pounded as he scanned the scene. Was that a silenced shot?

No — it was a bottle of champagne, bubbling all over a couple in the crowd on the main porch. Cruz ripped his gaze back to the side terrace, where the curtain flapped. The woman was gone.

She's safe! Safe! His tiger cheered.

He turned back toward the hit man, who'd also been distracted from his shot by the pop.

Destiny smiles on her, his tiger hummed.

Cruz wasn't so sure, because the second man kept his rifle high, squinting through his sights, intent on finding the woman for a second chance. Cruz sniffed for his scent, but the man was upwind.

Can't let him kill her, his tiger cried.

Cruz couldn't understand why it felt so important to keep that woman safe. But it did, and within the space of two heartbeats, the urge went from a vague feeling to a burning need.

Must keep her safe. Must get her away from this place! his tiger screamed.

Cruz cursed, disassembling the rifle in seconds flat, wondering what the woman had to do with the other shooter. Then he zipped the weapon into his bag and took off, racing through the woods with feline stealth. Within a matter of minutes, he'd concealed the rifle, plucked a stray leaf from his hair, and climbed the stairs to the golf club, straightening his tie as he went. He hated suits — and crowds — but he'd worn his best tux tonight so he could fit in if necessary. A good soldier always had a Plan B, right?

He'd find the woman, get her someplace private, and search for the truth in her eyes. Then he'd decide who to kill — the woman or the armed man in the woods. He could sense those preying eyes sweep the party as clearly as he might see a searchlight making regular sweeps.

That woman is mine, he told himself, trying to mask his rage at the imposter.

That woman is mine, his tiger hummed in a totally different tone.

Books by Anna Lowe

Aloha Shifters - Jewels of the Heart

Lure of the Dragon (Book 1)

Lure of the Wolf (Book 2)

Lure of the Bear (Book 3)

Lure of the Tiger (Book 4)

Love of the Dragon (Book 5)

The Wolves of Twin Moon Ranch

Desert Hunt (the Prequel)

Desert Moon (Book 1)

Desert Wolf: Complete Collection (Four short stories)

Desert Blood (Book 2)

Desert Fate (Book 3)

Desert Heart (Book 4)

Desert Yule (a short story)

Desert Rose (Book 5)

Desert Roots (Book 6)

Sasquatch Surprise (a Twin Moon spin-off story)

Blue Moon Saloon

Perfection (a short story prequel)

Damnation (Book 1)

Temptation (Book 2)

Redemption (Book 3)

Salvation (Book 4)

Deception (Book 5)

Celebration (a holiday treat)

Shifters in Vegas

Paranormal romance with a zany twist

Gambling on Trouble

Gambling on Her Dragon

Gambling on Her Bear

Serendipity Adventure Romance

Off the Charts

Uncharted

Entangled

Windswept

Adrift

Travel Romance

Veiled Fantasies

Island Fantasies

visit www.annalowebooks.com

Free Books

Get your free e-books now!

Sign up for my newsletter at *annalowebooks.com* to get three free books!

- *Desert Wolf*: Friend or Foe (Book 1.1 in the Twin Moon Ranch series)

- *Off the Charts* (the prequel to the Serendipity Adventure series)

- *Perfection* (the prequel to the Blue Moon Saloon series)

About the Author

USA Today and Amazon bestselling author Anna Lowe loves putting the "hero" back into heroine and letting location ignite a passionate romance. She likes a heroine who is independent, intelligent, and imperfect – a woman who is doing just fine on her own. But give the heroine a good man – not to mention a chance to overcome her own inhibitions – and she'll never turn down the chance for adventure, nor shy away from danger.

Anna loves dogs, sports, and travel – and letting those inspire her fiction. On any given weekend, you might find her hiking in the mountains or hunched over her laptop, working on her latest story. Either way, the day will end with a chunk of dark chocolate and a good read.

Visit AnnaLoweBooks.com